Among the Hunted

Among the Hunted

Michael Hammonds

DOUBLEDAY & COMPANY, INC.

GARDEN CITY, NEW YORK

1973

All of the characters in this book
are fictitious, and any resemblance to actual persons, living or dead,
is purely coincidental.

First Edition

ISBN: 0-385-01103-2
Library of Congress Catalog Card Number 72–96241
Copyright © 1973 by Michael Hammonds
All Rights Reserved
Printed in the United States of America

For my wife, Jane
who saved me from my own spelling

Among the Hunted

ONE

The train pushed over the rise and began its descent away from the mountains and toward the town.

Marshal Gabe Early shoved the side door of the mail car open, and leaning against the frame, he raised his pale blue eyes to look back at the dark peaks. Rain clouds shadowed them, blending them into breathing mist, making it seem like they weren't really there at all, but something he'd imagined.

His eyes still on the mountains, he shoved his coat aside, and reached into his vest pocket, fishing out a plug of tobacco and a silver-handled knife. He cut himself a chew and slipped it beneath his graying mustache with the blade of the knife.

"Not long now," he whispered to himself, fingering the plug and the knife back in his vest pocket.

"What?"

Gabe glanced back around at Harry Keegan's questioning face. He'd almost forgotten the federal marshal there beside the express shipment.

"Nothin'," Gabe shook his head, "clearin' my throat."

Smiling knowingly, Keegan lifted his wiry frame out of the chair and looked back at the mountains too.

"Thinkin' about your place?"

"Some I guess," Gabe admitted.

"Mexico," Harry nodded, "what's the name of that place?"

"No name really," Gabe said. "Place in the mountains down there below Crucero Vado." He looked forward, nodding once, "We're comin' in to Bitterroot. Don't guess those cowhands gave Mitch too bad a time—"

Harry shook his head, "You worry about that deputy of yours too much."

Gabe glanced back around sharply, then hauled the door shut. "I'll take a look forward in the passenger car."

The U.S. marshal frowned at being cut off. "You do worry about him too much, you know."

"See you in a minute," Gabe said, and walked through the platform doorway. He crossed to the next car and went inside.

Gabe surveyed the passengers quickly. He'd done it once when they'd started from Santa Fe, and nothing much had changed. The car was nearly empty. Farmer and his wife. Faces hard and staring, strangely twinlike in their stiffness, as if the dust and sun had stamped them. A cowhand. Man in a suit. Drummer sitting across from a young woman.

Gabe took notice of that. The drummer had been sitting back at the other end of the car at the beginning of the trip. The woman's eyes glanced around to touch Gabe's for a moment, then jerked away to look out the window. She didn't seem to be paying much attention to the drummer.

Gabe remembered her from the last time he'd been up. Red-haired and damn near six feet tall, but she wasn't big. Looked like a seed-filled buffalo hunter's best effort at fantasy.

The drummer leaned forward, toward her, and she seemed to press back against the seat.

Frowning tiredly, Gabe strode forward and leaned against the seat, staring down at the drummer until he looked up. Sandy-haired with a fat red neck.

"Everything's fine here," the drummer said.

"I'm not the porter," Gabe said. "I'm the marshal of the town we're comin' into."

The drummer swallowed.

Gabe looked to the woman. "And her husband."

The drummer swallowed again. "Ma'am," he nodded hurriedly, dragging his case up and moving away to the other end of the car.

Gabe looked back to the woman, and touched the brim of his hat.

The woman smiled almost painfully. "Thank you, Marshal."

"Husband shouldn't let you travel alone, Mrs.—"

The red-haired woman touched her cameo frowning. "Miss," she corrected him, "Jenny Shannon. I'm not married."

Gabe felt the tug of a smile.

"That's too bad," he touched the brim of his hat again, and walked off down the aisle.

Still holding her cameo, Jenny Shannon watched the man wearing the badge go through the door, then turned her eyes back out the window. It was all so barren, she thought, as the town came toward her. The town was like a part of the dust itself. Tired and struggling. Even the hills being lush with spring didn't help her feeling of waste. Perhaps it was because there was so much of it, and so few buildings.

The town rose up beside her, filling the windows as the train began to labor and draw slowly into the station, its whistle blasting. Her hand touched the cameo again, and looking down at it, she pulled the hand away.

Standing, she pulled her bag from under her seat. It would be all right, she told herself. It would be all right.

The shrill of the train whistle jerked Deputy Mitch Prentice's eyes up, and he almost dropped the pistol he'd just jerked from its holster.

Glancing around self-consciously, he looked at the clock over the door of the marshal's office. Two-thirty. He'd been practicing his fast draw longer than he'd thought. Looking at the gun in his hand, he smiled. Didn't matter about the time. He was getting good. Very good. He'd forgotten to do a couple of things around town, but—

The whistle sounded again, and he placed the empty gun in the drawer of his desk, then stood for a moment trying to think of what he needed to do the most.

Remembering the tray he'd left in the prisoner's cell, he rushed back through the cell block doorway and into the dark adobe cocoon.

On the bunk in the cell, Silas Toomey wobbled his head around.

"What's that?"

"Train's comin' in," Mitch smiled. "Gabe's on it."

"Oh," the man on the bunk groaned, then looked up, eying the boy. "Won't be able to play at being lawman no more."

"Ain't playin'," Mitch frowned, and backing out of the cell, he slammed the door.

The man on the bunk barked in agony. "Careful, boy, careful. Noise. When am I gettin' out of here?—"

"Gabe'll let you know," the deputy said, and walked back into the office of the jailhouse. He placed the tray on the table next to the pot-bellied stove and pushed his blond hair back out of his eyes.

The whistle of the train sounded again, and this time Mitch frowned, glancing around the office. He hated to admit it, but he was a little sorry Gabe was back. It would be good to see him and all that, but he enjoyed having the responsibility of taking care of the town. 'Course, not much had happened. Just Toomey and another fella getting drunk.

Mitch picked his hat off his desk and walked to the door, then hesitated. He'd liked it, though. He knew he would because it was what he'd always wanted. "What the hell," he shrugged. His time would come. And stepping out of the office, he locked it and hurried down the street to meet Gabe and Harry Keegan.

Riding in from the north end of town, Zach Harper saw the train pull into the station, then Mitch Prentice walking to meet it. Early was back. A frown showed through Harper's dark beard as he reined up in front of the Ace-High Saloon.

Dismounting, he glanced back in the direction of the station and tied his horse.

"Damn," he whispered tightly, then crossed the walk and pushed into the saloon.

"He's upstairs," the bartender said, and nodding, Zach went up to the second floor. The hall was dusty and seemed to slant to one side.

Zach walked to the first door and hit it.

"What?" a deep voice roared, and the rancher smiled at the indignation.

"Get up, Ald," he said.

"Go to hell."

The door jerked open suddenly. Zach's partner. Ald Stacker, turned back into the room. He wore only his pants.

"Jesus, Zach," he complained, and sat down in a chair. A Sharps stood next to the chair. A woman rustled in the sheets of the bed, still asleep. Zach brought his eyes back to his partner. Ald had his shirt on and was stomping his feet into his boots. The woman in the bed turned again. Finished, Ald stood, gathered in his Sharps, and placed a ten-dollar gold piece next to the woman's head.

"Think I'd get lost?" he grumbled at Zach as they started down the stairs.

"Lot of work to do," Zach shrugged.

"Never was any good at ranchin'—" Ald mumbled, reaching the bottom of the stairs.

"Bullshit—" Zach smiled.

They crossed the room to the bar.

"Gonna go back to huntin'."

"Bullshit."

Stacker stared at Zach for a moment, then surrendered a sigh. "Yeah," he nodded. "Man can't hunt for a livin' no more. Gettin' civilized," he snorted, and slammed his hand down on the bar. "Whiskey," he growled.

The skinny bartender brought them a bottle and left it with two glasses.

Stacker downed one quickly and poured another.

"Gotta buy that whiskey farm," he sighed.

"You've had two days in town, Ald. You ready to come back out?"

Stacker looked surprised. "Two days? Damn," he grinned amazedly. "Musta had a good time." Downing another drink, he slapped Zach on the back. "All right," he nodded sourly, "let's go back to work."

They turned to the door.

"Two days, huh?" Stacker cocked his head as they went through the doorway and onto the sidewalk. "Well—" he nodded, then stopped abruptly, his hand tightening on his Sharps.

A hard frown pulled Stacker's mouth.

"Sonofabitch," he whispered. "It's Gabe Early."

"He'll be gone in a few days. Just . . . let it go . . ."

Stacker's eyes jerked back to Zach. "He slugged me, Zach. Drunk or not, he shouldn'ta slugged me."

"Let's go home, Ald, we've—"

"No," Stacker answered, looking back down toward the train station. "I ain't runnin'."

"Who said anything about runnin'? We were headed—"

"When I'm ready," Stacker hissed. "Goin' down to the Holman House. You comin'?" he asked, and stepped into the street and was walking before Zach could answer.

Watching his partner, Zach shook his head. Stacker and his goddamn temper. It had taken Zach a long time to overlook it.

"Hell," the bearded man sighed, and untying his horse, he followed Stacker up the street.

Woody Sizemore stood at his hotel window and watched the men in the wagon as they unloaded the strongbox from the train. Pushing his bowler hat back on his head, he smiled and turned back into the room.

A shoulder holster and coat hung on the chair beside his bed.

He slipped the holster on, checked the .45, then holstering it again, he pulled the coat on. Straightening his tie in the mirror, he smiled again.

"Just like a garter salesman," he mused, and adjusted the well-cut coat. Lifting the bowler, he pushed his hair back from his broad face, then went downstairs to the first floor of the Holman House. At the bottom of the stairs, he turned through the swinging doors and into the saloon.

Squinting in the dim light, Sizemore glanced around the room. A couple of penny-ante card players, cowboy at the bar. His gaze stopped on a mule-faced man sitting alone at a table near the door. The man looked up as Sizemore came across the room and sat down. Sizemore poured himself a drink from the bottle on the table and tasted the whiskey.

"Tell 'em to come in, Candy," Sizemore said quietly. "It's here."

TWO

Gabe and Harry Keegan watched as the four men from the express office finished dragging the strongbox from the mail car to the flatbed wagon they had backed up to the door.

"Must weigh five hundred pounds," one of the four men pulling it complained.

"Close to it," Gabe nodded. "They didn't want some cat-eyed fella throwin' it over his saddle too easy."

One of the men climbed into the driver's seat and pulled away into the street as the other three sat down wearily in the back.

"Well, that's done," Keegan said in relief, and looked at

Gabe. "You can collect your money from the express company. That's the nice thing about bein' a town officer—"

Gabe picked up his saddlebags from a corner and tossed Keegan's to him. "How's that?"

"You get paid for this trip. Us federal boys have to do this for a livin'."

"Ridin' trains and gettin' soft ain't a bad life, Harry." He jumped from the mail car to the ground. Keegan followed him.

"Soft, hell," the U.S. marshal grumbled. "Put in more hours in the saddle, while you sit on your ass in that saloon playin' cards—"

"Hello, Harry—Gabe—" Mitch Prentice interrupted, approaching the two men.

Gabe turned and smiled, "Mitch—" he started and saw Ald Stacker coming up the street. The hunter hesitated in front of the Holman House and looked at Gabe. Then, turning, he went into the bar.

Gabe looked back at the deputy. "When you let him out?"

"Day after you left, like you said."

Gabe nodded sourly. "Still mad as hell," he sighed, and looked at the boy. "How'd it go?"

"Not bad," the deputy shrugged.

"Any trouble?"

"Not really. That preacher you warned about sellin' that medicine of his—"

"Toomey?"

"Went to drinkin' some of it himself and doin' a sermon in the middle of the night on the balcony of the Ace-High to some of the girls." Mitch shook his head, "And he wasn't tryin' to save 'em."

"And him a preacher, too. . . ."

"Anyway, I let him rest last night, you can—" the deputy's words trailed as he stared past Gabe to the station platform.

Gabe looked back over his shoulder. Jenny Shannon stepped off the train, put her bags down for a moment, and seeing the marshal, picked them up again and walked down the steps to him.

"I wonder if you could tell me where the hotel is?"

"Right there, ma'am." Gabe pointed out the Holman House.

"Thank you," she said, and turning, walked away down the street.

Mitch watched with wide eyes and a half-open mouth.

"Mitch—"

The deputy's eyes jerked back to Gabe.

"What?"

"Anything else?"

"No," the deputy shook his head. "Not much . . . you know, she was sorta pretty."

"Sorta," Keegan coughed.

Gabe smiled. "Do me a favor, Mitch."

"Sure—"

"Go down to the express office and collect my money from Dooley for me, and see that that strongbox is locked up."

"Right," the deputy nodded, and turning, walked back down the street, his eyes roaming to the woman still walking toward the hotel.

"Be over at the Holman House," he yelled after the boy, but the deputy didn't hear him. "Damn," he sighed.

"That money puts you over the top, don't it, Gabe?"

Gabe looked back to Keegan, "What—"

"For your place—"

"Oh," Gabe nodded. "Yeah."

The two men started down the street.

"Headed out tomorrow?"

Gabe cleared his throat, and nodded to the north, "Don't know, Harry," he said. "Looks like rain. Been thinkin' I might oughta hang around a couple of more days. . . ."

"Crap," Harry frowned. "It's that damn kid."

Gabe's mouth hardened, "Don't know what you're talkin' about."

"You been coverin' for that kid, Gabe."

Gabe stopped. "Harry—" he began, then shook his head, "he's just a kid like any other kid. I'm leavin' in a couple of days, and the kid'll be the law till the new man comes." He stretched and sighed. "Hell," he grumbled, "I'm gonna go up to my room, then take me a bath. Where you gonna be?"

Keegan nodded toward the bar, "Crackin' the leather in my throat."

Gabe went into the hotel and Keegan pushed his way into the saloon. Stacker was at the table, Zach at the bar buying a bottle. Keegan crossed the room and leaned on the bar.

"A long one," he called to the bartender, then shifting his eyes to Zach, he nodded.

"Harry," the bearded man acknowledged him.

Keegan glanced over his shoulder. "Ald still riled?"

"Yeah," Zach nodded coldly, "he's got a right to be."

Frowning, Keegan shook his head. "He was doin' his job."

"His way of doin' things is always the hard way."

"Sometimes," Keegan nodded slowly, "sometimes there ain't the time for it to be any other way—"

"Time, hell," Zach snapped, then, breathing deeply, was calm again. "Seems like there could've been another way of doin' it other'n sluggin' him. Ald liked him," he shook his head, "ain't right to do a friend like that."

Picking up the bottle off the bar, he nodded, "Have a good stay," and carried the bottle back to Stacker's table.

Keegan turned back to the bar and sipped his drink.

"Honor," he whispered, and shook his head.

Zach was a funny one, the U.S. marshal reflected. He was fiercely loyal to his men and expected the same from them. Almost like he was trying to make them family. Smiling wearily, he lifted his glass slightly. "To honorable men," he said sourly, and finished the drink.

THREE

Jenny Shannon checked into a room at the Holman House and went upstairs. Pulling the shades, she took off her jacket and blouse, placed her cameo on the washstand, poured water, and washed her face, shoulders, and hands. She dried herself and opened her bag to find a fresh blouse. Taking the blouse out, she saw the letter from Edwin Williams again.

She picked it up and held it for a moment. She had done that several times during the past few days. Just held the letter. Three months ago she had seen his advertisement for a tutor and a governess for his son. She had written and was hired by mail.

And she was finally free.

She placed the letter back in the suitcase, and picking up the blouse, she put it on and buttoned it. She turned to the door, then looked back to the washstand.

Frowning, she picked up the cameo off the washstand, and opening it, looked at the picture of her father inside. Stiff, was the word that immediately came to mind. He had given her the cameo on her eighteenth birthday, the same day he'd told her that he'd arranged for her to marry a man named Stephen Griffin.

She snapped the cameo shut, and slipped it around her neck. Neither of them had come to the station to say goodbye when she had left for New Mexico. Maybe it was just as well. She would go to this place called Hatchet, and finally be free of them. That was all she really wanted.

Picking up her handbag, she left the room and went downstairs. At the desk she asked directions to the stagecoach office.

"Right across the street," the clerk pointed through the door.

A small, thin man of about thirty, with worried eyes, looked at her as she came in.

"Yes . . . ma'am?"

"I want to purchase a ticket on tomorrow's coach to Hatchet." She brought her purse up and opened it.

The agent nodded, "Yes, ma'am. Be three-fifty. But there ain't no stage to Hatchet tomorrow."

Jenny hesitated, "When is the next one?"

"Well," the agent cleared his throat, "let's see now," he scratched his head, "Wednesday."

"Wednesday!" she exclaimed. "That's six days."

"Yes, ma'am. Six days."

"I can't wait six days," she closed her purse. "Is there any other way to get to Hatchet?"

"Not unless you can sit a horse, or if somebody's headed down that way."

"Do you know of anyone traveling in that direction?"

"Toward Hatchet. No, ma'am," he shook his head. "You might ask the marshal, though. Might know. Office is right up the street there," he pointed back up the street across from the Ace-High Saloon.

"Thank you," she nodded, and left. She walked up the street to the marshal's office. The door was locked. Frowning, she crossed the street back to the hotel.

Sitting on the porch of the Holman House, Woody Sizemore watched the woman as she walked around town. For the first time that day, he thought about something other than the express office, and then only fleetingly. When she walked past him quickly and entered the hotel, he eased his eyes back to the express office. Business was business, and that came first.

He stood up from his chair, stretching his long legs out

stiffly and tipping the bowler hat a little farther back on his head, and glanced to the north end of Main Street expectantly.

He took his watch from his pocket. Fifteen after six, he frowned. They were late.

Sighing tightly, he looked back to the express office. One of the shades was being lowered. Closing time!

Sizemore stepped hurriedly off the sidewalk and into the street. The shade began to move downward in the next window, and Sizemore had to think to keep himself from running. He should have been across the street five minutes ago.

Stepping up on the sidewalk, he opened the door of the express office, nearly hitting the man inside.

"I was just—" the agent started.

Sizemore smiled. "Just wanted to get a ticket for Santa Fe."

"Santa Fe. Now?" the agent's worried eyes jerked to the safe behind the counter. "Mister, I—"

Sizemore moved away from the window, toward the counter.

"Hate to do things at the last minute," he said, the agent's eyes following him.

"Listen, mister—"

Away from the door, and in the protection of the drawn shades, Sizemore turned, reaching under his coat, lifting out the .45, thumbing the hammer, and leveling it at the agent.

The skinny man's eyes widened.

"Jesus," he whispered, "I told them—"

"Quiet," Sizemore was still smiling, "or I'll blow you straight to hell, friend."

The agent shook his head. "You can't—"

"The hell I can't," Sizemore growled. "Now finish pulling those shades and open that safe. Unless you think it's worth dyin' for."

Gabe and Mitch stepped out onto the porch of the Holman House in the twilight. A breeze touched them, and Gabe glanced up north, smelling rain. The sun was nearly gone, rustling shadows and gold light. Stepping into the street, they ambled toward the office.

Mitch glanced toward the express office. Dooley, the agent, was pulling down the last of his shades.

"Lot of money," the deputy mused.

"Lot of money," Gabe nodded. "Enough to set a man wantin'—"

"Like that place of yours?"

"Like that," Gabe nodded.

Mitch was silent a moment, then, "Now come on, you never settled down before. Got a place, I mean."

"Had one once. Long time ago. Let it go. Lost it because I didn't have the money to hold onto it. Took me awhile to get enough to go back."

"Not me," Mitch shook his head. "Always just wanted to be a lawman. Somethin' excitin'."

Gabe hesitated and stopped, turning to the deputy slowly.

"Ever occur to you you might get killed?"

Mitch rustled his shoulders. "I guess."

Gabe nodded, "There's a lot more to this than the excitement." He smiled, "How's your draw? Still practicing?"

Mitch cleared his throat. This was still a sore spot with him. Two weeks before he'd been practicing and put a bullet through his boot, slicing one toe. Gabe had nicknamed him Toe-shot, then, and bought him a new pair of boots.

"Didn't hear you," Gabe's grin widened.

"Yeah, some," Mitch nodded grudgingly.

"Want another lesson?"

Mitch smiled. "Right now?"

"Right now," Gabe said, and glanced around. A sparrow landed on the weather vane of the livery. "On the livery—"

Mitch opened his hands, relaxing like Gabe had taught him.

"Now," Gabe barked, and the boy spun, drawing his Colt, bringing it around to the top of the barn, thumbing the hammer, then jerking the shot off to one side.

"You missed," Gabe said.

"There was a bird up there," Mitch explained, "I—"

Gabe shook his head. "That's the whole point. It was the bird you were supposed to hit."

Mitch holstered his gun. "What the hell's the use of that?"

"None," Gabe said, "but in this business you don't think about killing. You do it before somebody has a chance to do it to you."

Mitch frowned. "I'll learn," he said. "It just takes time."

Gabe shook his head. "You know," he said, walking again, "used to know a fella up around South Pass City, Wyoming. Lucky Callahan. Bad sonofabitch. Hung out in one of the saloons. Musta whipped about thirty–forty men, somethin' like that. Anyhow, when somebody'd go to paintin' their nose with whiskey, he'd go lookin' for Lucky." Gabe stepped up on the porch of the office. "Stomped a mudhole in all of 'em. All but one. One fella that went after him cold sober." Gabe shook his head. "He knew how to do it. You ain't ready for Lucky Callahan yet, son. Won't be till you admit you ain't no killer."

Mitch gazed up at him and blinked. He didn't say anything for a long time.

"I know what I want, Gabe."

Gabe nodded, "All right, son," he sighed. "Let's let those folks out of their cells."

The rattle of hooves jerked Sizemore's eyes from the agent opening the safe to the door.

"Keep workin'," he said quietly, and backing across the room, he lifted the shade on the door a crack.

The mule-faced man, Candy, and Bob Graffman dismounted. Graffman carried his sadddlebags. The two men strolled up on the porch, and Sizemore jerked the door open. The two men stepped inside quickly.

"Hi, Woody," Candy grinned.

"Where the hell were you?" Sizemore snapped.

Candy's grin faded. "We was—"

"He lost his watch, boss," Graffman cut in.

"Damn," Sizemore growled. He jerked his head toward the door. "Candy, get those horses someplace else."

"Right, boss," Candy nodded, and hurried back out the door.

"That it?" Graffman looked at the safe.

"That's it," Sizemore smiled.

The nervous agent finished with the combination, and opening the safe, stood up.

"Don't . . . know," he stuttered, "what good it'll do you— can't move it."

Sizemore motioned him aside with his gun.

"Have faith," he said, and glanced at Graffman. "Bob, what you think?"

Graffman walked behind the counter and to the safe. He looked at the strongbox inside.

He grinned back at Sizemore, patting his saddlebags.

"No problem," he said.

The cell block was dark. It was always dark. The walls were made of thick adobe, making the cells cavelike. They smelled of vomit and urine and a dank heaviness. Gabe felt himself tremble as he stepped toward the cells. He didn't like their smell or their darkness.

Two figures rustled.

"Time for church," Gabe said, unlocking the door and leaving the close walls, emerging back into the office.

A cowboy squinted into the light, a trace of a frown on his lips. He brushed off his small frame and stretched.

"Worst jail I was ever in," he shook his head and headed for the door.

Silas Toomey was next. A traveling preacher, he called himself. He came from the darkness of the cells like he'd been resurrected through horseshit with his mouth open. He was wearing his black broadcloth suit, but most of the dignity had been wrinkled out of it.

"Marshal," he said with his preaching voice, "I protest this—"

Toomey," Gabe said, "you gotta quit drinkin' what you sell."

"I—"

"Especially in this town."

Toomey cleared his throat, "Well, I can certainly tell when the law is prejudiced. There are other places. Coulter or Hatchet should welcome me."

"Coulter's too big," Gabe shook his head. "Hatchet'll be your place."

"Why, thank you, Marshal."

"Just not here," Gabe said, and Toomey's mouth wagged shut.

"Yes," he nodded, "perhaps not."

Tipping his hat, he rushed out the door.

Mitch sat down on his desk and laughed. "Oh," he reached into his pocket, "before I forget it again, I guess I should give you the money from the express company." He pulled an envelope from his jeans and handed it to Gabe.

Gabe took it, nodding. "Helps," he said.

He looked up, eying the boy for a moment. "Why . . . don't you start rounds without me tonight, Mitch. Got some paperwork to do."

"Right," the deputy nodded, and adjusting his hat, he ambled out of the office and down the street.

Gabe walked to the window and watched the boy checking doors and peering in darkened windows. The lawman turned back to his desk shaking his head. Goddamn that Harry Keegan, anyhow. . . .

"Damn," the marshal grumbled.

Harry had been right as rain. The funny thing was that Gabe hadn't realized it until Harry had said it. He was covering for the boy. He had been ever since he'd hired him six months ago. The boy was no lawman, and he had tried to keep him from getting killed until Mitch realized it. He had thought about firing Mitch, but that would do no good; the boy would have just gone someplace else to get a job. He should have left a long time ago, but the boy had gotten in the way of it.

Gabe sat down at his desk and looked at the money on his desk. Turning in the chair, he opened the safe behind his desk and took out a small strongbox. It wasn't locked. He lifted the lid and looked at the money inside. More than five thousand dollars. Enough for a place of his own.

Funny thing was that was how it had all started. Him and getting a place of his own. And a girl named Allie.

He had homesteaded a place near Sheridan, Wyoming. A place with good pasture, pasture so green it looked like you could put your hands in and they'd come out as green. He was supposed to marry Allie twenty-two years ago this spring and settle on that land. But it had been a bad spring. Rustlers and night riders had been stealing everything they could get their hands on. Gabe's small herd had been all but wiped out in one night. He'd gone to town to borrow money, and found you had to have money to borrow it. He got a job as a deputy. He bought a handgun and learned how to use it. He learned well and found that he was good at the job, and he liked the excitement.

Allie had disapproved, but he stayed at the deputying job anyway. It was coming on winter and there was no way he could make it on his place. Just a little more money, he'd told Allie, but after a while it didn't do any good to talk to her anymore. . . .

Allie would have children now. Gabe took his silver-handled pen knife from his pocket and turned it in his fingers. Children, he nodded, sons. . . .

He blinked and looked at the money. Now he had the chance to go back and start over again. Have the land he wanted. And he was letting the boy get in the way of it.

"Damn," he grumbled aloud, "how'd I let that boy get so close to me," he shook his head, "and why?"

He put the money into the box and put it back into the safe, and locked the safe.

He had done all he could for the boy; now it was his time. Time to go home. He finally had the passage, and he was going. Headed south. Down to that little village in the mountains. Get a place and run some cattle. Fish the high streams. Take it easy. Three days south of the Rio Caballo. Four if he had to go through Crucero Vado, and most likely he would have to, because of the rain. The only crossing on the Rio Caballo was at Crucero Vado.

Six days, then. Two to Crucero Vado, and four on down to the mountains.

Sizemore and Graffman tied the express agent, shoved him into the back room, then went back to the safe and the huge strongbox inside.

"Sure you can blow that thing without levelin' the town?"

A smile parted Graffman's ruddy face. "Woody," he sniffed confidently, "you seen me work."

Sizemore nodded. "All right." He pulled his watch from his pocket and handed it to the dynamite man. "Remember, wait till four, then—"

Graffman glanced at the strongbox eagerly. "Why not just go ahead—"

Sizemore shook his head. "Because at four everybody'll be asleep. And we can ride out of here north in the dark, then circle back south to Crucero Vado come daylight."

"All right," Graffman agreed half-heartedly.

Sizemore turned to the door.

"And no lights in here."

"Graffman nodded.

Sizemore parted the shade, and seeing it was clear, opened the door and crossed the street back to the Holman House porch and his chair.

FOUR

The rap of boots on the walk outside brought Gabe's eyes around. The door opened and Jenny Shannon came into the office, followed by Mitch.

"This is the—"

"We've met," the woman said, leaving the deputy and striding across the room, walking like she had enough gravel to go up against the whole Sioux nation. But her eyes gave her away.

"Perhaps you can tell me how to get to Hatchet," she nearly demanded. "It seems that there isn't another stage-coach for a week."

Gabe shook his head. "No way that I know of, unless you can ride."

"No," she frowned, "I never learned."

"Wish I hadn't," Gabe smiled. "Couldn't go it alone any-how—"

"Too bad Toomey ain't runnin' a coach—" Mitch broke in.

The woman turned, "Toomey?"

"Preacher," Mitch explained. "Headed down there, but—"

"Where can I find him?" she asked.

"Miss Shannon," Gabe frowned, "ole Toomey ain't the sort that you should be travelin' with. He's—"

"I'll decide that. Where might I find him?"

"Wagon's at Legate's Livery," Gabe sighed, then he looked at her. "What is it?"

She blinked, "What?"

"What makes it so all-fired important?"

Jenny swallowed stiffly, "I just—I have to get—there—thank you, Marshal." She turned and nodded to Mitch, "And you, Mr. Prentice."

She hurried through the door, and Gabe watched her as she turned down the street. He turned to Mitch, frowning.

"Sometimes I wonder if I taught you anything at all."

"I was just tryin' to help," Mitch said.

"I know," Gabe nodded wearily, "I know."

"Pretty as—" he cocked his head. "Damn."

"And a runner," Gabe said. He took his hat from his desk and put it on. "Watch the office," he said. "I'm gonna do a turn around the town."

Jenny Shannon hurried down the street toward the sign over the livery stable. Legate, a small, white-haired man, sat in front on a box smoking a pipe.

"Yes'um," he nodded, "that fella Toomey's got his wagon here, right through there in the wagon yard."

Jenny walked past the old man.

"And tell him he's got work to do if he ever plans to leave this town," Legate called after her.

She walked on through the barn and out into the wagon yard. A wagon stood at the far end beside a creek. The back of the wagon was covered with a wooden shell, which was rounded on the top. On the side of the wagon, written in flowering script, was,

"Brother Silas Toomey," and under it, "Follow me . . ."

From Matthew, she nodded. Chapter Nine, verse nine. Follow.

A fire burned at the rear of the wagon, and a tall man sat on the tailgate, shoulders bowed, a cup of coffee trembling in his hand.

"Mr. Toomey?" she probed, and the man remained in the same position, a great shock of black hair hanging limply toward the cup.

Walking closer, Jenny said his name again, "Mr. Toomey?"

and his head bobbed up, eyes rimmed in red jerking toward her. Drops of coffee splashed darkly onto his pants leg and into the dust, jeweling into pools.

"Oh," he said, squinting at the woman. "Oh," he said again.

"Are you in pain, Mr. Toomey?" Jenny asked.

"Yes, ma'am," the preacher nodded.

Jenny walked around by the fire. It felt good in the cold night air.

"Is there anything that can be done?"

"No, ma'am," Toomey muttered, raising his face. His face was very deep and gaunt. He looked more like a shadow than a man. He pulled his lips apart. "Far as I know they ain't no cure for a hangover—"

"Mr. Toomey," Jenny cut in.

"Yes, ma'am?"

Jenny drew a measured breath. "I've come to ask you a favor."

Toomey stared blankly. "Me, ma'am?"

"I understand you're going to Hatchet?"

"Yes, ma'am," the preacher nodded.

"I—" she hesitated, "I'd like to go with you."

Toomey blinked. His eyes dropped to her waist and came up again. Slowly. When his eyes came up to hers they were blank again.

"I'm sorry, ma'am. Would you mind saying that again?"

"I'd like to go with you," Jenny repeated patiently.

Toomey shook his head incredulously, "Me . . ." he looked up. "What about the stagecoach?"

"There is none until next week."

Toomey nodded, "Ma'am. Ain't you worried about your reputation? I mean, well, you know what I mean."

"You're a man of God, Mr. Toomey."

The dark man placed his cup down on the tailgate.

"That's . . . true . . . ma'am . . . but . . ." he shook his

head, "I got enough troubles. I got a bill I have to work off
here—"

"I have some money, Mr. Toomey, I can pay it for you."

Toomey looked up for a minute, and shook his head again.
No, ma'am, just wouldn't work."

Watching her walk away, Toomey growled a deep sigh in
his throat.

Why the hell did she have to come to him? He didn't want
to do her or anybody else any favors. He especially didn't like
strangers in his wagon.

He looked back around at it. It was all he had, and he
didn't like people around it. Picking up his coffee cup, he
smiled faintly.

With any luck he would have worked off his bill for
Legate by tomorrow and he would be able to leave the next
day. That would put him in Hatchet Saturday night, and
ready for Sunday morning. Folks were always ready for a
preacher on Sunday morning, and liniment oil the rest of the
week. And in a one-street town like Hatchet a good traveling
preacher could make enough not to have to work for a
while. Pamphlets and medicine oil. Enough to stay free
awhile longer.

He sipped the coffee and felt a little better. A day of work
and then moving on. That's all he really wanted.

Getting up, he tossed the rest of the coffee into the dirt,
and crawled into the back of his wagon.

It was like a very small room inside. A bed on one side.
Small trunk. A box of liniment oil. Mirror hanging on the
wall. Two doors led through to the driver's seat. It had been
home now for a lot of years.

Sitting down on the bunk, Toomey glanced around the
interior and picked a bottle out of the box. He uncorked the
bottle and took a sip.

Everything a man would need, he thought, looking around
the wagon. Everything, he nodded, and taking another sip

from the bottle, he frowned slightly. Everything but good whiskey.

"Oh well," the preacher sighed, and lying back on his bunk, he sipped more from the bottle and tried not to think about having to work tomorrow.

Jenny walked back through the barn, across the street, and up to her room. Sighing, she sat down on the bed, and looking down, saw her hands trembling.

"Foolish," she said to herself, "that's foolish."

Her shoulders rustled against the darkness of the room and a web of hopelessness, a feeling that her father had been right. That she couldn't do anything on her own. Her hand came up to the cameo around her neck, and realizing she was fingering it again, she pulled her hand down.

She lay back on her bed. She had to get to Hatchet. She had to get to Hatchet to prove she could finally do something on her own. She closed her eyes, and her hand fluttered to her throat and the cameo.

She would find a way. She had to.

FIVE

Gabe found Harry Keegan in the Ace-High. Walking toward him, he saw Zach Harper and Ald Stacker at the bar. Stacker was heavy with drink and sagging against the bar.

Frowning, Gabe turned to Harry and sat down at his table.

"That Stacker?" Harry asked as Gabe rested into his seat.

"Afraid so," Gabe nodded.

"Gets a little mean, don't he?"

"A little." He hesitated for a moment, then, "Just wanted to say so long, Harry. I'm headin' out early in the mornin'."

Harry smiled nodding. "Don't blame you. I never liked long goodbyes either. Gettin' it over with quick." He watched as Gabe hesitated again, pulling his knife and a plug of tobacco from his vest pocket. "What is it, Gabe?" he finally asked.

"Nothin'. Just keep an eye on the town, and—"

"The boy?"

"Mitch?" Gabe looked up and shrugged, "Yeah, you might keep an eye on him too." He slipped the chew into his mouth and stood up, putting the knife and plug away. "Take care, Harry," he winked and turned away.

Gabe had taken two steps when he saw the movement in the corner of his eye. A man coming hard.

Sidestepping, he hit the man in the jaw, twisting him sideways, then crashing to the floor. It was a moment before he realized it was Ald Stacker.

"Goddammit," he growled.

On the floor Stacker lifted himself to his knees.

"Stay down," the lawman snapped.

Shaking his head, Stacker pushed himself back up slowly, then dived suddenly for Gabe's legs, driving them both back against the bar. Kicking one leg free, Gabe kneed the hunter in the side of the head, ramming him into the wood of the bar. Stacker slumped down and Gabe followed him. Stacker was going down and he knew it, but the marshal hit him again.

A hand grabbed his arm from behind, twisting the lawman around, and turning, he drew without thinking, thumbing the hammer and jamming it into Zach Harper's stomach.

Harper looked at the gun, then raised his eyes.

"Killing season?" he asked, the anger quieting his voice.

Gabe looked down at the gun, aware for the first time that it was in his hand.

Releasing the hammer, he holstered it.

He looked at Stacker.

"He's a lucky man," Gabe said to Zach, and turning, walked out the door and into the cool air.

He looked down at his hands. They were trembling. Someone came out behind him, and he looked around. Harry Keegan came out on the walk, shaking his head.

"What the hell were you doin' in there?"

Gabe shook his head. "I don't know, Harry. Mad about somethin', I guess. I shouldn't of done that." He shook his head again. "Night, Harry," he said, stepping off the boardwalk.

"Gabe," Harry called after him.

The lawman looked back.

"I'll keep an eye on him for you. Don't worry about the kid."

Gabe started to say something, then nodding, he turned away, silent, and walked down the street.

Leaning forward in his chair, Woody Sizemore watched the marshal come out of the Ace-High and up the street.

The rattle of hooves at the north end of town eased his eyes around. Two men rode in and down the long street.

Sizemore pulled a cigar from his pocket and struck a match on the arm of his chair. He lit the cigar slowly, rolling it in his mouth, the glow reddening his face. He tossed the match into the street as the two men rode by him past the livery, down a small drop in the street to the Ace-High.

Sizemore propped his feet against the porch support, and easing himself back, he looked at the marshal again. Gabe had walked by the livery and stepped onto the boardwalk. The lawman was good at his job, Sizemore noted. Kept to the shadows, his eyes continually moving.

Two more men rode in from the south by the marshal and pulled up in front of the Holman House. Four, Sizemore nodded, dropping the legs of the chair back to the porch. Four more yet to come.

The marshal mounted the steps of the hotel as Sizemore stood up from his chair. He nodded to the lawman.

"Nice town," Sizemore said.

Gabe nodded, "If you like towns."

Sizemore smiled at the lawman, squinting to see his face. He liked to know an enemy's eyes. "I know the feeling."

"Here long?"

"Few days. A little business to take care of."

"Hope it's profitable."

Sizemore nodded. "It will be."

"Night," Gabe said, and moved on past the well-dressed man and into the hotel.

Sizemore looked across the street at the express office. "It will be," he nodded, and sat back down.

Gabe was on the stairs headed up to his room when he saw Jenny Shannon at the desk, talking to the night clerk. The night clerk was shaking his head, and Miss Shannon was frowning. She turned away from the desk.

Gabe hesitated, then against his better judgment, he walked back down the stairs. Maybe it was her eyes.

"Miss Shannon," he touched the brim of his hat.

She turned and nodded.

"Yes?"

"Just wonderin' how you made out with Toomey."

Her eyes fell, and she shook her head. "Not too well," she said softly, then raised her eyes determinedly. "I'll try someplace else tomorrow."

"Toomey's kind of contrary."

"I offered to pay his bill there, and he still wouldn't take me."

Gabe worked his jaw, getting another squeeze of tobacco juice.

"He owe a bill?"

"Yes," she nodded.

"Wait here a minute, ma'am," Gabe said, and walked back out the door and down to the livery.

Gabe walked through the livery to the wagon in the corral and pounded on the door.

"What is it?"

"Marshal Early."

There was a sound of groaning, then the wagon rocked slightly, the door opened, and Toomey leaned precariously toward him.

"What might I do for you, Marshal?" the preacher said in his best diction and stiff breath.

"Been at your stuff again?"

"Feeling ill."

Gabe nodded. "There was a woman here before. Red-haired."

Toomey smiled.

"If I pay your feed bill will you take her along?"

Toomey frowned.

"A woman?" He shook his head. "Don't want no strangers in my wagon, Marshal. Especially a woman. What the hell do I want with a woman . . . well, you know what I mean."

Gabe nodded. "You're gonna have to work your bill off, you know that, don't you?"

"I'm perfectly aware of the matter."

"And you'd rather work than take a woman along for one day?"

Toomey weakened for a moment.

"I . . ." he looked back into the wagon. "Yes," he nodded his head. "Don't want no strangers in my wagon, Marshal."

Gabe stared at him a moment.

"All right," he nodded, and turning, walked back into the livery. The inside of the barn was lit with one lantern. Gabe squinted around.

"Fred?"

"Yeah," the old man came out of his room and up the aisle toward Gabe. "Just doin' dinner."

"That preacher," Gabe nodded back over his shoulder, "how many days he gonna owe you?"

"Ahh," Legate scratched his behind, "one, I guess."

Gabe took a five-dollar gold piece from his pocket and handed it to the livery man. Legate took it questioningly.

"Work him like hell," Gabe smiled, "and tell him he owes you another day tomorrow when he's done."

Legate smiled, then sniffed, "Ain't too kind."

"Good for the soul," Gabe winked, and walked out of the barn.

Jenny Shannon was where he left her. She stood up when he came in the door.

"You'll likely have a way to Hatchet tomorrow night, ma'am."

She smiled suddenly.

"You're very kind, Marshal."

"No," he shook his head, "no, ma'am, I ain't. I wish I was."

Touching the brim of his hat, he left her in the lobby and went upstairs to his room.

In the express office, Bob Graffman examined again the dynamite he'd cut, the fuse, and the lock on the strongbox. His long hands were careful and precise. Nodding, he sat back against the counter and looked at the watch again.

Ten-thirty.

"Damn," he muttered. It had to be more than ten-thirty. He brought the watch closer to his face in the darkness.

It read the same.

"Damn," he sighed, and examined the dynamite, fuse, and strongbox again.

Across the street, Woody Sizemore watched the last two of his men ride in. Standing up, he nodded to them, and they turned their horses into the alley beside the hotel.

He looked back at the clock in the lobby of the Holman House.

Eleven-twenty.

Turning, he walked down the porch to the bar, and inside. Candy was at the bar. Only a couple of hangers-on left. Big man with a Sharps across the table. The bearded man with him looked bored. The big man was getting mean, talking loud.

Sizemore bellied up to the bar next to Candy. "Make sure ever'body knows where they're supposed to be," he said. "I'll be up in my room."

SIX

Gabe was up at three-thirty.

Shoving the blankets aside, he climbed out of bed and walked to the window. It would be light in an hour or so.

The town was dark. Shadow and form. A gathering of time and dust. Funny, he cocked his head, that he felt little for it. He had never felt a part of it, like he belonged here, but then he'd never felt that way about anyplace. Just the mountains a long time ago when he was young. And being young had been a long time ago. He would be forty-eight years old come this fall.

He looked back at his room. There was nothing to show that he'd lived there for ten years. He learned a long time ago not to try to keep things that slowed him down.

"Certain way of doin' things," he sighed. It was time to move on.

Dressing quickly, he packed most of what he owned into

his saddlebags, and the rest in his bedroll, then went downstairs and into the cold morning. It had rained a little during
the night, muddying the streets. To the north, heavy clouds
darkened the mountains and stars.

Gabe hesitated on the porch of the hotel and glanced up
the street, his eyes on Mrs. Ford's boarding house, where
Mitch had a room.

He wished now he'd said goodbye to the boy.

"Damn," he grumbled, frowning at himself for being soft,
and walked down the street to his office. He put his hand
in his pocket for his key, then saw the door was open a
crack. Drawing his pistol and easing the door open, Gabe
stepped inside.

Mitch was asleep on the office bunk.

Gabe closed the door and frowned.

"Gonna get yourself killed, Toe-shot."

A lawman never slept in his office, he'd told Mitch that
before. Makes him too easy to find. And he never leaves the
door open.

"Hell," the lawman grumbled, and shaking his head, he
crossed the floor quietly to his safe. He took the money from
the strongbox, then finding a piece of oilskin in his desk, he
wrapped the money in it and shoved it into his saddlebags.

Turning, he walked to the door and looked back at the boy
on the bunk. "So long, Toe-shot," he whispered and went
back out the door and locked it behind him.

He walked down the short incline to the livery, and finding
his bay, he saddled him. He took his slicker from his bedroll
and tied it across the bedroll so he could get to it quickly
if it rained.

Mounting his bay, he saw Toomey's wagon in the yard and
smiled. He was a little sorry now he'd be causing the preacher
a bad day, but there were other things to be sorrier about,
he sighed, and his mouth lost the smile. Stacker, for one.

That was done now.

He turned his horse out of the barn and headed him north.

He rode down the main street and up the hill out of town. At the top of the hill, he reined the bay in for a moment and looked back. Just a town, he nodded, and pulling the bay around, he spurred him out toward Mexico.

Hearing the sound of hooves below, Woody Sizemore walked to his window and watched Gabe Early ride out of town.

"There's one thing goin' right, Candy," he said to the mule-faced man behind him, and turning, he slipped his coat on. "Let's go."

They walked out of the room and down the hall two doors and knocked. The door opened immediately and a Mexican stepped into the hall.

"Get the others, Jesus," Woody said to the Mexican, and hurrying to the stairs, went down them quickly. The clerk was asleep behind his desk. He rustled slightly as the men went by and out the door.

"Get the horses, Candy," Woody ordered the mule-faced man, then stepped into the street, crossing to the express office.

Candy mounted his horse, and leading two other horses, crossed behind them.

The Mexican emerged from the back door of the hotel. Three men followed him to the horses tied at the hitching rail; mounting, they divided into twos and rode around the back of the hotel and up the separate alley on both sides of the building.

Seeing them in position, Woody Sizemore hesitated in front of the express office. Another man was on the balcony of the Holman House. Two more were in alleys to the south.

Sizemore smiled, and turning, he knocked on the door.

It opened slightly, and he stepped inside.

"Now," he nodded to Bob Graffman.

The click of a door closing rustled Mitch Prentice in his sleep. It took him a long time to open his eyes. Pulling his long legs around to the side of the bed he dropped them, glancing around the room.

"Gabe?" he called, and stood up. Shrugging, he walked to the window to see if he was on the street. He knew he'd heard that door close.

The street was empty. He was turning away when two men came out of the Holman House. One walked off down the street. The other, a man in a bowler hat, crossed the street to the express office.

"Funny," Mitch narrowed his eyes and watched as the man in the bowler knocked on the door, then went inside.

From up the street, the other man he'd seen led two horses down the street and stopped in front of the express office. Mitch turned back to his bed, slamming his boots on and jerking a Winchester from the wall. He checked the rifle, and picking up his gunbelt from his desk, he strapped it on.

Turning, he went to the door. His hand trembled on the knob, and for a moment he didn't think he was going to be able to open it. Grasping it harder, he swallowed his lead-heavy breath and eased the door open.

He stepped onto the sidewalk. The heaviness bled through him, weighting his feet and hands, swelling his bladder. He had to force himself to walk, holding the rifle up, keeping his eyes concentrated on the express office a block away down the street. The man on the horse hadn't seen him yet, and Mitch moved faster.

Stepping into the street, Mitch ran, crossing to Miles's Hardware Store, hitting the wall hard. Swallowing, he edged a look around the side of the building. The express office was the next building down. The man on the horse still hadn't seen him. Levering his Winchester, he started around the front of the building, and the wall exploded in front of him.

Gabe started down a small canyon, and hearing something like thumps behind him, he jerked his bay to a halt. He knew the sound of shots. Steadying his animal, he tried to pick out a direction. Another grouping tapped the wind, filtering down the canyon. They were from town. Gabe took the bay back around. "Toe-shot," he whispered, spurring the animal, giving him his head, strapping him hard.

Mitch reeled back around the building, slipping in the mud, hitting on his knees. Another shot shattered the corner above his head, showering him with wood. Shoving himself back against the wall, he pushed himself to his feet.

A slug pounded into the wall, spiking wooden needles into his face. Shaking his head, he swore, "Sonofabitch—"

Where the hell was he?

He heard the shot this time. Above him. On the balcony of the hotel.

Jamming the rifle back around the corner, he pumped five shots toward the balcony and jerked back around the corner. Someone fired at him from the express office, but the firing from the hotel had stopped. Turning away from the street, Mitch ran to the back of the hardware store to the alley running behind it and the express office. Drawing his Colt, he took a quick look. It was clear.

Rounding the corner, the deputy felt a sudden kick of air, like he'd run into something. Then he heard the explosion. From the express office.

Mitch ran the length of the hardware store, and pressing himself against the wall, he took a quick glance at the express office. All he ever really saw was the .45 coming up in the man's hand, a bowler hat behind it someplace. He reeled back around the building as two shots smashed wood into splinters. Two more shots tore chunks out of the corner, driving Mitch back.

Resting his rifle against the wall, the deputy changed his pistol to his left hand, then nosing the barrel around the corner, he thumbed off three shots. The .45 barked again and again, erupting planks into a holocaust of wood and lead.

Harry Keegan charged down the stairs of the Holman House, his gun in his hand. A man clamored in front of him, slipping down the stairs, gripping his pistol and bolting across the lobby through the front door.

"Hey," Keegan screamed at him, but the man was already on the porch, standing up, raising his pistol and firing one shot.

"The hotel," he heard one of the outlaws yell and slammed to the floor beneath a window as a shock of lead exploded across the porch, hammering the man on the porch back through the glass of the hotel door.

Pushing himself up, Keegan got a quick shot off through the window, then ducked. Another volley of fire tore over the porch, shattering glass and wood.

"Damn," Keegan muttered. There were people firing all over the place. Too many to know how many there were. Or get a clear shot at.

Boots pounded on the stairs behind him, and rolling over, Keegan brought his pistol up as Zach Harper and Ald Stacker rushed down the stairs.

"Get down," Keegan shouted at them.

Crouching down, both men crawled toward him. Harper was still in his underwear, trying to blink the sleep from his eyes. Stacker was still fully dressed, and even at a foot, Keegan could smell the sleep-soured whiskey on his breath.

"—the hell's goin' on?" Harper asked, trying to see out the window.

"Express office," Keegan answered quickly. "Go through the bar," he said to Zach, and Harper was moving.

Stacker raised his Sharps and put a shot through the window.

"Get to that other window," Keegan said.

"Don't tell me what to do," Stacker barked, and turning, growled, "I'm gonna get me some—" and he was on his feet, staggering down the back hallway.

"Damn," Keegan shook his head, then taking a glance through the window, he saw a man running down the far side of the street. Getting off two quick shots, Keegan slammed the man through the hardware store window.

A slug pounded into the wood of the frame next to him, and turning his gun, he fired across the street. Two men ran from the side of the express office into the street. Keegan sighted on the first man and knocked his leg from under him, sending him somersaulting into the dust, Keegan jerked back the hammer of his gun to finish him, but rifle fire from down the street drove him back down.

Behind the hardware store, Mitch heard the men running from the express office and stepped into the open. The man with the saddlebags was on the ground, and the man with the bowler was helping him up, shoving him into the saddle.

Mitch ran across to the express office, using it for partial cover, firing once at the men on foot and missing.

Suddenly there were two more men in the street on horseback.

Stepping clear of the building, Mitch tried again to hit the men scrambling onto their horses, but there was too much movement, and he couldn't get a clear shot.

A shot kicked up mud next to his foot. Another ripped past his ear.

Turning, he started running back for the express office door but slipped, sprawling in the mud as shots peppered the wall above his head.

Pulling his eyes up, he could see the men riding. He got his legs under him and ran to the end of the alley, but it was too late to hit anything now.

Keegan rushed out onto the porch of the hotel.

"Get to some horses," he shouted at the deputy.

Mitch blinked at him with glazed eyes.

"Now," the U.S. marshal snapped.

Nodding, Mitch felt his legs moving numbly, then running, and he was stumbling down the street toward the livery.

A rider burst from the barn and Mitch thumbed the hammer of his pistol, then lowered it as Ald Stacker came toward him riding hard, letting out a whoop.

"Let's get to it," the hunter shouted, hammering by the deputy, grinning as he strapped the horse out.

Mitch turned to watch him and felt something wet on his face. Looking up, the deputy frowned.

It was beginning to rain.

Riding hard through the rain, Gabe pulled up in front of his office, and without tying his horse, rushed inside.

Harry Keegan was taking a rifle from the wall. His eyes jerked to Gabe as he came in the door.

"Left early, I take it?"

Gabe nodded.

"Keep ridin', Gabe, this is none of your concern."

"Where's the boy?"

"Down in the livery." He nodded slowly, "He's all right," then smiled. "Did just fine."

"Express office?"

Harry nodded. The sound of horses outside brought both their eyes around. Mitch slammed through the door and stood staring at Gabe.

"Where were you this mornin'? Hell," he grinned, "you missed it all."

Gabe cleared his throat. "I . . . was outside of town. Checkin' on something."

He turned back to Keegan. "Who've we got to ride?"

Harry frowned. "Gabe—"

"Who have we got?" Gabe's jaw hardened.

Keegan looked to the boy and back to Gabe, and shaking his head, he surrendered, "Not many . . . spring roundup and all. . . ."

Zach Harper burst in the door. "We'd better get a move on. Ald's out there someplace."

Gabe turned. "Alone?"

Zach frowned, shrugging, "He was still a little . . . anyway, he rode out after 'em. Excitement, I guess."

"Christ," the old lawman grumbled, and looked back to the boy.

"You stay here," he ordered him.

The boy opened his mouth to protest, but Gabe stopped him. "They could double back," Gabe said. "Hit something else. Bank, maybe."

He looked at Keegan. "Ain't that right, Harry?"

Keegan swallowed. "Yeah," the U.S. marshal nodded, "could happen."

"Let's go," Gabe said, pushing by the boy and out the door.

Gabe, Harry Keegan, Zach Harper, and two cowhands of Harper's, Coy Spanner and Tom Bennett, rode out north.

SEVEN

Gray, sparse light wandered rain shadows through the dim hills and blurred mountains. Gabe walked a mile out of town, following the tracks until he had enough light to see the ground from horseback.

Five miles north of Bitterroot the tracks had nearly disappeared in the wash of rain.

Spitting water, Gabe shook his head. "We're losin' 'em."

"Think they're headed for that run of canyons?" Keegan asked.

Gabe considered it a moment. "No," he answered, "they're moving north. These tracks have been makin' a long turn."

"You think they might be headed back to town?" Keegan asked, remembering what he'd said to Mitch.

"No," Gabe said. "Swinging too wide. Might as well fan

and see if we can't pick up their tracks." He pointed north.
"Zach, you and your boys head up that way. Harry, you
might as well keep goin' west, and I'll trail off south. Meet
back at town tonight. And don't anybody try to take 'em
on alone. You see 'em, come on back to town."

Zach stared back at Gabe. "Thought you were due to quit
this job."

"I'll pick my time, Zach."

The bearded man nodded, "Hard to quit somethin' you
enjoy, ain't it?" He jerked the head of his black around hard
and headed him out, his men following.

Gabe watched them ride off, then brought his eyes back to
Keegan. The U.S. marshal was shaking his head.

"What in the hell are you doin' anyhow, Gabe?"

"Tryin' to come up with those boys."

"Bullshit," Keegan sighed. "You know that's not what I'm
talkin' about."

"Harry, we ought to—"

"Quit tryin' to live that boy's life, Gabe. Get the hell out
of here while you can. Ain't many of us get out of this line
of work breathin'—"

The old marshal felt the words and winced.

"Maybe that's it, Harry. I'd like to leave somethin' behind
more'n just dead men. . . ." He looked up at his friend,
"Lot of 'em you know, Art French back there in Oklahoma
saved my bacon. I can show you Bill Wintergreen's blood
stains back there in Bitterroot where he bled to death on the
sidewalk. Lawdogs. Fools," he whispered.

"Good men," said Keegan.

"Yeah," Gabe nodded. "Well, at least I kept the boy out of
this one." He shook his head, "Maybe my havin' a place will
do it. Workin' the land again. Take a look around and head
out again tomorrow."

"What is it about that boy anyhow?"

Gabe pulled his horse around, "See you back in town,
Harry. Buy you a drink."

Keegan watched him ride away, and smiling softly, he nodded, "Fools . . ."

Gabe rode south across the rocky ground, then into a crisscrossing of arroyos. It was hard country, made worse by the rain.

He rode the rest of the day, riding at angles, cutting a wide swath, and the longer he rode, and the more cold the rain chilled into him, the more he thought he was not only a fool, but a damn fool. He should have kept riding this morning. Tomorrow, he nodded. Tomorrow, he was headed for home, even if the whole goddamn town blew up. He was headed home.

Twilight mingled with the rain as he eased his bay down a creek bed and through a stand of aspen. The stage road was about four miles from here if he remembered right, and from there it was ten or twelve miles back to town. Get a couple of hours' sleep and—

He reined the bay in hard and stood alert in the saddle. He'd heard something in back of him. The rattle of hooves on stone.

He turned the bay's head back around and dismounted. The whisper of rain and the rushing of the creek mixed, webbing through the white-barked trees. Squinting into the blending of trees and rain, Gabe caught an echo of movement. Slight, but there. And the clatter of hooves again.

Gabe drew his gun from beneath his slicker, and leaving his horse behind, he slipped into the trees. The false darkness thickened in his eyes, making halves and shadows of everything. Ahead, Gabe could make out a clearing. A horse stood in it. The man was on the other side, kneeling down, examining the horse's right front shoe. A rifle rested on the ground next to him.

Gabe stepped through the trees, thankful for the sound of the rain and the creek. He tried to make the man out in the twilight but couldn't. He was big, that was all he was sure of.

Gabe moved around the high end of the clearing, trying to

get the horse out of the way. When he had a full view of the man, he stepped around a tree and his boot came down on a small branch. Leaves rattled. The man's head jerked up, his hand jutting out for the rifle beside him.

The lawman moved before he thought, bringing the gun up, thumbing the hammer and firing, slamming a slug square into the man's back, kicking him forward into the water, the rifle dropping from his hand.

"Damn," Gabe growled, rushing across the clearing. Leaning down to pull the man from the creek, he saw the rifle that had fallen from his hand. A Sharps.

"Jesus," Gabe whispered, reaching out, grasping the man's shoulder, leaning him out of the water and back on the bank. Ald Stacker stared up at the lawman, eyes blinking, his mouth working against a paste of blood that seemed to be strangling him. Stacker trembled in his hands, then his jaw stopped moving. His eyes were fixed on Gabe.

"Oh . . . goddamn," the lawman murmured, sitting back on the bank. He took off his hat, shaking his head. "Goddammit all anyway, Ald . . ." he whispered, the words thickening his throat. He hadn't meant to kill Stacker. He'd've shot him in the shoulder if there'd been a split second more. Or if he'd had time to think.

It was as if he'd had nothing to say about it. He'd taught himself a long time ago not to think about the killing. Just to hit and stop what moved. Like he'd tried to teach Mitch yesterday in the street when he'd missed the sparrow.

He looked at his gun again. He'd taught himself well. Now he had nothing to say about it. Nothing at all.

Resting his gun in his slicker, Gabe reached out, pushing the wet hair from the dead man's face. "Never even bought your whiskey farm," he sighed.

Another dead man to remember. One who had been a friend.

"Hell," he whispered, tasting salt in the rain on his face.

EIGHT

Fred Legate shook his head heavily, looking at the exhausted form of Silas Toomey slouching on the edge of a watering trough in the livery yard. A grimy pitchfork was at the preacher's feet.

"Ain't much at work, are you, Reverend?" the livery man said sourly.

"Ain't much at slavery," Toomey sighed.

"Well," the livery man mopped his face with a stained hand-kerchief, "you only got one more day of it."

Toomey's head jerked up. "One more day," he coughed. "You old sinner, you said one day and I've—"

"Now," Legate raised his hand calmly, "by all rights I could take that wagon till you paid me what you owe me, now if—"

"No," Toomey shook his head in surrender, "don't do that. I'll work it off."

Legate sniffed, "Just that you ain't work 'nuff for a two-year-old baby girl," he cocked his head. "You're kinda slack, boy."

"Legate," Toomey pleaded, "I gotta get to Hatchet by to-morrow night so's I can get set up and get to preachin' Sunday mornin'. I'll send you the money."

"Man don't go 'round leavin' due behind him," nodded Legate. "What's right is right," he orated, and slapped the preacher on the back. "See you in the mornin'."

Toomey watched Legate walk off down through the barn and into a part of it he'd made into a home for himself.

Toomey stood up with difficulty and wandered through the

coming twilight across the yard and back to his wagon. He laid down on his bunk inside and sighed. Another day.

If he just had a little money. A little. Enough to get into a poker game. Just—

He blinked and sat up remembering Jenny Shannon. "I'll pay you," she'd said.

"No," he said aloud and laid back down. "No," he said to himself again.

It had been a murderous day. Cleaning the stalls had been the worst part. The shovel, the pitchfork, and then the honey-wagon to the edge of town. Then shoveling it off.

And he would have to go through it again tomorrow. Horses weren't known to let up any in their bowel movements from one day to the next.

"Oh! Lord," he sighed. But he knew he was done for.

Toomey walked down the hallway of the Holman House, turned and went back to the stairs, then turned around again and walked back to the number the clerk had given him. He knocked lightly. No answer. He hit it again. No answer. The third time he gave it three good raps.

From inside a voice was muffled by the wood: "Yes?"

"Miss Shannon?"

"Yes?"

"Toomey, Miss Shannon."

A hesitant "Yes?"

The traveling preacher glared at the door. "Miss . . . Shannon . . . I don't feel like talkin' to the numbers on this door. . . ."

"I've retired for the night, Mr. Toomey."

"Miss Shannon—"

A large form emerged from the door to Toomey's left.

A man starkly resembling a bear stood gazing out of a mass of hair (a beard and forelock hanging).

"You hurrahin' the lady, friend?" he growled.

Toomey shook his head and tried smiling.

"Then how come all the noise?"

"Well, I was just—" Toomey forced the grin back on his face.

"What's so goddamn funny?"

"Nothing," Toomey forced the grin off his face.

"You sure you ain't hurrahin' that lady?"

"Sure," Toomey nodded.

The bear stalked down the hall in his long handles and hit Jenny Shannon's door.

"Lady?"

"Yes?"

"He hurrahin' you, lady?"

The door opened a crack.

"Why no," Jenny said through the slight opening.

The bear shifted his dark eyes back to Toomey, "Well," he grumbled. "All right," he nodded, and stalked back to his room.

"What did you want, Mr. Toomey?"

Toomey shifted his weight from one foot to another.

"Can I come inside, ma'am?"

"I'm in my nightclothes, Mr. Toomey." She watched him shift his weight again. "Is something the matter?"

"No . . . no," he shook his head, squeezing his kidneys a little harder, and that made it worse. "Ma'am, the Lord works his wonders in strange ways—"

Jenny Shannon's face brightened, and it all seemed worth it. "You mean you'll take me with you?"

Toomey smiled and then was suddenly angry with himself. "Yes ma'am, but I'm afraid I'll have to ask you for about three dollars for my feed bill."

"All right, Mr. Toomey, I'll pay you in the morning." She smiled. Toomey frowned: "Well, yes, ma'am, goodnight then." He nodded and walked away.

The bear's door opened a crack.

Toomey smiled, "Take heart my son: Your sins are forgiven. . . . Why do you think evil in your heart? For which is easier to say: 'Your sins are forgiven' or to say, 'Rise and walk'? But that you may know that the son of man has authority on the earth to forgive sins . . . rise, take your bed, and go home. . . ."

A confused set of eyes followed him as Toomey walked down the hall.

"Thanks," the bear said.

Mitch Prentice sat at his desk, feet propped up, watching the street and frowning. He had waited all day for something more to happen. Nothing did. He knew nothing would. Lifting his feet from the desk and dropping them to the floor, he shifted in his chair and scratched his leg.

"Hell," he grumbled. New jeans always itched for a while. He'd have to wash out those others he'd been wearing that morning.

Standing, the deputy ambled to the window and looked out awhile. Then, taking his hat, he strolled into the evening street to do his rounds. The rain had let up an hour before but had left a chill and a good smell behind.

He was in front of the Ace-High when he heard the rattling of hooves coming in from the north. Stepping into the street away from the light, he was able to make out four riders. Keegan, Harper, and Harper's two men. An aching hollowness twisted in the deputy's stomach, and he looked back up the street for Gabe. He had to keep himself from running as he walked out to meet the riders.

"Find anything?" he asked Keegan.

The U.S. marshal wagged his tired head. "Not even a buffalo turd."

"Seen Stacker?" Zach asked him.

"Stacker?" Mitch said confusedly, "Oh . . . damn, I forgot about 'im. No, I ain't seen him, Zach."

The big rancher frowned and looked around to his men. "Might as well stay the night."

The two cowhands smiled. "Stay the night," the taller one nodded. "Thanks, boss."

"Buy you a drink," Zach said, turning his horse toward the Ace-High.

Keegan turned his animal toward the livery. Mitch hesitated and followed him in. Keegan had already dismounted as Mitch came through the door and down the stalls.

"Gabe. . . still ridin' around out there?"

Keegan paused as he undid the cinch, then nodded, "Suppose so. Don't worry, son. Gabe knows his business." He pulled the saddle off the horse and heaved it up on the side of the stall.

"Yeah," Mitch agreed.

Keegan took the bridle from the horse and hung it on the wall. "What made you want to go to lawin' anyhow, boy?"

Mitch shrugged, "I dunno . . . excitement, I guess. . . ."

"In this town?" The U.S. marshal haltered his animal.

"Bitterroot used to be pretty lively."

Keegan came out of the stall. "Till Gabe came."

"Yeah," Mitch nodded, "but there are some other places. California."

Keegan smiled, pushing his hat back on his head.

"Places. . ." he mused, and looked at the deputy. "Still got it on everything else, don't it?"

"Mostly," the boy nodded.

"Come on," Keegan slapped him on the shoulder, "I'm gonna have me something hot. You eat yet?"

Mitch reddened slightly, "Sort of forgot . . . but I better not. I got rounds to do."

Keegan smiled again, nodding, "All right, son, you do your rounds. Find me later and I'll get you drunk," he said and walked away.

Mitch wandered out of the barn after Keegan. "Places," he nodded, it was a good word. That's all his father had ever talked about. Places. And worked his life away busting horses for two dollars a throw. Always saving so they could go to

those places. Then one day a horse kicked him in the head and
they buried him in a dusty town with no name. Mitch blinked.
He was going to do better than that.

Turning and looking around, he started his rounds.

NINE

It seemed like he'd been riding a long time when Gabe finally
saw the lights of town. Somehow it didn't do much good. Not
even the rain letting up did much good.

Leading Stacker's horse with the dead man across him, Gabe
came up the long street into town, reining up in front of the
undertaker's.

He dismounted, and crossing the boardwalk, he pushed
through the doorway.

The undertaker, Sid Coffee, was sitting at a makeshift desk
eating a sandwich. He looked up and smiled at seeing Gabe.
He stood up, wiping his hands on his fat belly.

"Customer?" he looked past Gabe anxiously.

A coldness ground Gabe's stomach. He didn't like Coffee.
Maybe it wasn't Coffee, but the fact that he made his money
from dead men. But then again, so did he.

Gabe stared at the undertaker like a twisted reflection, then
jerked his thumb over his shoulder.

"On the horse."

Coffee belched pleasurably, "Right."

"And Sid—"

"Yeah, Gabe?"

"Make sure that horse gets across to the livery this time."

A pained look flickered Coffee's eyes, "Why sure, Gabe. Who is it—"

Without answering, Gabe turned and walked back into the night air. He stood staring at the dead man. His arm had caught on the stock of the old Sharps. Gabe walked to Stacker and lifted his arm down, then remembering Coffee, he slipped the rifle from its scabbard, and taking the cartridge belt from around the saddle horn, he wrapped it around the stock and pulled the buckle tight.

"I'm goin' home, too, Ald," he whispered, and turning, he took the reins of his bay and led him down the street to the livery.

He led his bay into a stall. Legate came from his room.

"Howdy, Gabe."

"Fred," he nodded.

"Done like you asked."

Gabe looked at him questioningly. "How's that?"

"The preacher," Legate pointed toward the wagon in the corral. "Worked him like a sonofabitch—"

"Oh," Gabe remembered, "yeah."

"Gonna pay me in the mornin'. Says he's gettin' the hell outta here and never comin' back," Legate laughed, slapping his leg.

Gabe smiled wanly. "No tellin' what two days'da done for him." He pointed to his bay, "Grain him, but leave the saddle on him. I'm gonna need him later." He took the saddlebags, hooking them on his shoulder, and still carrying the Sharps, he thanked Legate and walked up the street to his office. Finding the door locked, he shouldered the bags, shifted the rifle to his other hand, and walked up the street toward the Holman House.

Coy Spanner stumbled out onto the porch of the Ace-High, belched, and looked down the street toward the Holman House.

"Bennett," he called behind him, and Bennett wandered through the swinging doors.

"Yeah," the cowhand answered.

"Let's go down to the Holman House."

"Ahm," Bennett groaned sourly.

"Got better women down there."

Bennett rubbed his chin. "I dunno, Coy," he shrugged.

Shaking his head, Spanner stepped into the street, and Bennett followed him reluctantly.

"Hey," Bennett tapped Spanner on the shoulder and stopped.

"What the hell is it now?—"

Bennett was staring across the street at the horse in front of the undertaker's.

"Ain't that Stacker's horse?"

Turning, Spanner squinted across the street, "Looks like him." Then he shook his head, "What would Stacker be doin' over at Coffee's?"

"I dunno," Bennett shrugged. "Let's go get that drink."

The two men started walking again, then Spanner hesitated. "Might ought to tell Zach."

"Jesus," Bennett grumbled, "wish you'd make up your mind what the hell you want to do."

Spanner turned back up the street. "Just think we ought to tell him—"

"Damn," Bennett sighed, following him back down the street.

Gabe pushed his way through the doors of the Holman House bar, then hesitating, his eyes moved over the room. Silas Toomey was at the bar nursing a beer. It was amazing how someone who was broke could always come up with beer money.

Seeing Harry Keegan at a back table, Gabe crossed the room and sat down opposite the U.S. marshal. He put the Sharps on the table.

Keegan glanced up and smiled.

"Don't know about you, but I had a nice day in the—" His eyes went to the rifle on the table. "Didn't know you had a Sharps—"

"Harry," Gabe interrupted him, "I . . . killed Ald Stacker," he said difficultly.

Keegan sat forward, nearly dropping his glass.

"You *what?*"

"I killed Ald Stacker." Gabe said it again, and the words seemed strange, like he wasn't really saying them and it wasn't really true.

"Why—"

"It was an accident. Came across him out there and was coming up behind him. Couldn't see him in the twilight, and he reached for his gun. I . . . just shot him . . . his hand moved and I pulled the trigger . . . it was reflex, I guess . . . something . . ."

Keegan shook his head bewilderedly. "God . . ." he whispered, "my God."

Gabe drew a hard breath. "You were right all along, Harry. I'm getting down south while I can. Before I kill anybody else. Shouldn't have come back—"

"Has nothin' to do with it," Keegan shook his head. "You did it for the boy."

"I was wrong in that too."

"I don't know, Gabe. Hell," he sighed, "it don't matter now."

Gabe shrugged his head. "I'm gonna find the boy. Say so long to him once'n for all. Gonna head out again in a few minutes."

"Tonight? Seems kinda foolish."

"I don't know, Harry," Gabe's hands tightened on the Sharps. "I have to . . ." he shrugged, "get free of this town. You know what I mean?"

Keegan nodded, understandingly. "I think so, Gabe." He stood up, "Mind if I walk with you a spell?"

Gabe smiled and pushed himself up.

"Cover my back, Harry."

Keegan grinned and stood up. As the two men started for the door he hesitated, "Hate to ask," he said, "but I don't suppose you came across anything of those boys who took the express office, did you?"

"Not a damn thing, Harry."

Keegan wagged his head glumly. "Neither'd anybody else," he sighed. "Helluva day."

"All the way around," Gabe agreed.

Zach Harper charged out of the Ace-High.

"Don't need you," he snapped to Spanner and Bennett, and stepping into the street, he had to think to keep himself from running across the street to Sid Coffee's. He strode out quickly, his chaps slapping against each other, echoing off the dark buildings.

He was half running, approaching Stacker's horse. Slamming past the door and into the empty office, he rushed to the half-opened door that led to Coffee's workroom.

Shoving the door open, Zach rammed into the room. Coffee jerked up straight from the body on the table.

"Zach—" he stammered, "what—"

The bearded man stared at Ald Stacker's body on the table, and unbelieving, walked toward it.

Leaning over the table, he touched the dead man softly. "You old—"

And his eyes stopped on the wound.

He looked at Coffee. "He's been shot in the back."

Coffee shook his head, trembling. "Zach, I—"

"Who shot him?"

Coffee swallowed trying to speak.

"Who, goddammit?" Zach raged, coming around the table, grasping Coffee's shirt, ramming him back into the wall.

"Who killed him?" Harper screamed.

"Gabe," Coffee choked, "Gabe brought him in. . . . Zach
. . . let go . . . Gabe . . ."

Dropping Coffee to let him sink to his knees, Zach turned,
running now, a whiteness raging in his bowels and eyes.

Throwing the door of the marshal's office open, he bulled
inside. Mitch Prentice looked up from his desk.

"Harper, what the hell—"

"Where's Gabe?"

"Still out—"

"He's back, where is he?"

Mitch shook his head, "I ain't seen—"

Zach turned back into the street. He waded into the mud.
He saw Keegan come out of the door of the Holman House.

Then Gabe. He was carrying Stacker's Sharps.

Gabe had just stepped out onto the porch of the Holman
House when he heard the shout.

"Early. You sonofabitch."

He turned, facing the man, his hand touching his gun. He
could barely make out Zach Harper standing in the street.

Keegan put his hand back to Gabe.

"Let me do this," he ordered, and looked back to the man
in the street. "It was an accident, Zach," Keegan called.
"There's no reason—"

"He shot 'im in the back. You couldn't even do it honorable, could you, Gabe. You had to shoot him in the back."
He moved his eyes to Keegan. "Get out of the way, Harry,
or I'll kill you, too," Zach shouted, walking up the street.
Behind him, Mitch came out of the marshal's office. Zach was
still walking. "Get out of the way, Harry," he screamed.
Keegan looked past the oncoming man. "Mitch," he called to
the deputy, "cover him."

Zach halted at the snap of a hammer being cocked.

"Now take his gun," Keegan ordered him. "Kill him if he
moves."

Mitch stepped into the street.

"Jesus," Gabe whispered, shaking his head regretfully.

"Zach," he called, stepping past the U.S. marshal, "it was like Harry said—"

"Bullshit—" Zach growled.

"Zach," Mitch warned him and coming up behind him, the deputy slipped his gun from its holster.

"Gabe—" Harry began.

"I owe him an explanation," Gabe barked and looked to Zach again. "It was dark," he tried to explain, "he went for his gun, and I didn't have the time—"

"Time?" the bearded man raged. "You always got time when it comes to killing a man."

Shaking his head, Gabe turned to Harry.

"It's no use," he sighed.

Harry's face was pale. "Let's go," the U.S. marshal said.

"All right," Gabe nodded, "I'm leavin'."

"No," Keegan said with difficulty, "I'm . . . takin' you in, Gabe."

"Let's go," he said.

"I told you—"

"You shot him in the back, Gabe—"

"I didn't have a choice, I—"

"You always got a choice about shooting a man in the back, Gabe." He shook his head, "Besides, I've got to hold you, you know that."

Gabe blinked, staring at his friend, then understanding, shook his head.

"I'm leavin', Harry, I'm goin'—" his hand gathered around the Sharps.

"Gabe—" Keegan's voice was harsh, his hand eased toward his gun.

Gabe rushed into Keegan, bringing the rifle butt up, hitting Keegan in the chin, slamming him stumbling back into the wall.

Falling, Keegan drew his gun, firing wild. The slug hit Gabe as he was turning, ripping a long swatch through his side, twisting him back into the wall. Grasping his side and the saddlebags, he pushed himself down the steps of the porch into the cover of the alley.

In the street Mitch took his eyes off Zach and started running toward the porch.

"Gabe—"

Wheeling, Zach rammed his fist into the deputy's stomach. Mitch doubled, dropping to the ground, and Zach jerked his pistol from his hand, then ran for the alley.

The pain from his side nearly dragged Gabe to his knees, but getting his hand against the wall, he pushed himself down the alley.

The sound of boots behind him pulled his eyes around, and drawing his pistol, he put three shots into the side of the building, then rounded the back corner of the Holman House.

"Spanner," he heard Zach shout, "down here."

Gabe could hear the harsh sound of running on the sidewalks. He looked at the line of buildings behind the Holman House that made up Howell Street. They would expect him to go that way. Besides, that's not where he needed to go. . . .

Scraping down the back of the hotel, Gabe came to the back door and stepped inside. The hall was clear. He could see the front door and part of the desk. Leaning against the backstairs bannister, he measured his breath through him, and wiped the sweat from his eyes.

He moved his bloody hand from his side and looked at where the bullet had ripped through his vest and shirt.

"Damn," he frowned. He'd just bought the shirt, and he was fond of the vest. He couldn't tell about the wound yet.

Down the hall, the front door rattled open. Gabe stepped up the stairs into the darkness.

Zach Harper charged across the lobby and looked down the hall. Turning back to the desk, he knocked on the door behind it.

"What—" a muffled voice answered.

Zach shoved the door open. In the darkness a man stirred on the bed.

"What the hell?"

"Johnny, you seen Gabe?"

"That you, Zach?"

"Have you seen Gabe?" Zach snapped.

"No, I—"

Zach slammed the door and walked back across the lobby and out onto the porch.

Mitch was helping Keegan to his feet. Zach glanced at them, then to the man standing at the end of the building.

"Bennett," he said, "go 'round back and tell Spanner to cover that door. Then you come back here. I'm goin' upstairs. And hurry."

The cowhand ducked around the side of the building.

"What's goin' on—" Mitch asked.

Keegan glared at him and picked up his gun.

"Thought you were coverin' him."

"I—" Mitch reddened.

"Yeah," Keegan frowned and pushed by the deputy toward Zach.

The bearded man squared his eyes on the marshal.

"Stay out of the way," he said.

"You want more people killed, Zach?"

"Just stay—"

"I can't do that and you know it. Now how's it goin' to be?"

Zach nodded. "You can come along. But when it comes down to it, I'm gonna kill him."

Bennett came back around the building and up on the walk.

Without saying anything, Zach turned and went into the hotel.

"Stay here," Keegan ordered Mitch and followed Harper inside.

Gabe came up over the landing into the shadowed hall. It was empty.

He turned toward his room, then hesitated and shook his head. He walked to the door and tried it. It was open. He fumbled in his pocket for the key, and fishing it out, locked the door. The next room was Jenny Shannon's. He touched the knob. He turned it. It held. He crossed the hall. The door was open.

He slipped inside and heard footfalls echo up the stairs. He closed the door, quickly, and made sure the room was empty.

Hurried footsteps came up the stairs and down the hall.

Zach Harper stopped in front of Gabe's door and pulled his gun. Keegan stood behind him.

Zach tried the door and looked back at Keegan. Keegan drew his pistol and nodded. Zach raised his foot and kicked the door open, leaving it hanging on its hinges. Zach stepped into the room, his gun sweeping it.

"Nothin'," he growled at Keegan, coming back out.

The door down the hall slipped open and Keegan caught a glimpse of red hair.

Another door swung open and a giant of a man stepped into the hall.

"What the hell is—"

"U.S. marshal," Keegan snapped, "get back in your room."

The big man did as he was told, and Keegan turned to the woman.

"Nothin' to worry about, ma'am. Just looking for a man."

"Oh," she nodded slightly, "do you have to be so—"

"You seen anybody?" Zach asked.

"No."

"If you do—"

"I won't," the woman snapped. "I'm leaving this town with Mr. Toomey tomorrow."

In the room across the hall, Gabe smiled wanly and lost it again as the footsteps came toward him. Drawing his pistol, he stepped behind the door and made sure it was unlocked. A fist hit the wood beside him. His breath sounded like thunder.

It was a wonder they couldn't hear him breathing downstairs. He pressed himself back against the wall as the knob rolled and the door eased open.

It stood open for a moment, then a fraction more. Gabe lifted his gun, leveling it at the edge of the door.

The light from the hall seemed to be stark bright, washing into the room.

The door hung open, its weight whispering in the hinges.

"Nothin'," Keegan finally said.

The door pulled to, and Gabe felt his hands trembling. For a moment he thought his knees would give.

The footsteps moved to the next door. Then the next. After some time he heard them going down the stairs again.

Zach and Keegan walked back out onto the porch of the Holman House.

"Bennett," the bearded man snapped at the cowhand standing next to the door, "Sumner and Willis were down in the Ace-High earlier. Tell Sumner to get down to the livery and Willis to the north end of town, Spanner, south, then you get out to the ranch and bring back everybody you can."

Bennett nodded and was running.

Down the porch, Keegan turned to Mitch.

"Come on, son," he said, "I want to have a look at Stacker."

The deputy shook his head. "Harry, you know Gabe. He wouldn't—"

Zach wheeled around.

"He would and he did, you goddamn pup."

Mitch started for Zach but Keegan grabbed his arm, pulling him back.

"There's been enough of that crap tonight." He pulled Mitch back down the porch. "Come on, dammit. You're the law here now. Act like it."

Mitch brought his eyes around meeting Keegan's, then nodding quietly, he stepped off the porch and into the street.

Keegan looked back to Zach for a long moment, then frowning, followed the boy.

Gabe walked to the bed, and easing himself down on it, he let the saddlebags drop, then set the Sharps against the wall.

Pulling his coat aside, he looked at the wound again.

"Damn, Harry," he whispered. He was going to have a helluva time sitting a horse. Especially running. The bullet had passed through without breaking anything. But still he was bleeding.

The sound of hooves brought his eyes up, and walking to the window, he parted the shade slightly and watched Tom Bennett ride north and out of town past a man at the end of the street. Shifting, Gabe peered toward the south end of the street. There was another man there.

Frowning, he walked back to the bed. Zach had it pretty well covered. Likely a man in the livery, too.

Stretching back against the wall, he looked at the wound and shook his head.

Question was, how the hell was he going to make it south?

Even starting now, the wound would slow him bad enough that Harper would find his tracks and overtake him before he made it to McAllister's.

Gabe stood up and walked to the window again and cracked the shade.

He needed time. Time to let the wound heal a little. Frowning, he shook his head. That was the trouble. He'd run out of time.

Below him a man wandered into the street and stumbled toward the livery, whistling, "Jesu, Joy of Man's Desiring." It was Toomey.

Gabe shook his head and started to turn to the bed.

Then he looked back into the street, smiling suddenly. "Brother Toomey," he whispered.

TEN

Zach Harper watched Bennett ride out of town strapping his animal hard, heading him for the ranch. In thirty minutes he would have ten to twelve men in town.

Nodding, Zach walked back across the porch and into the Holman House bar.

Cash, the bartender, was closing up. He stood washing glasses behind the bar.

"A bottle," the bearded man said quietly.

Cash hesitated, a glass in his hand. "I was just closin', Zach."

Zach lifted his eyes and stared at the bartender.

"Now," he said.

Nodding and putting the glass down, the bartender brought a bottle from beneath the counter and put it in front of Zach. He dried a glass and put it next to the bottle and left Zach alone.

The big rancher jerked the cork from the bottle and poured the liquid into the glass. Resting the bottle next to it, he let the glass sit for a minute.

"Whiskey farm," he whispered.

Cash looked up. "What?"

Zach shook his head. "Nothing," he said, and picked up the glass.

Ten years ago a big raw-boned hunter had picked him out of the middle of a fight in a saloon in Fort Carson, Colorado. They had fought their way to the saloon door, then the hunter had lifted that bigger-than-hell rifle and blown out a light, and they made it into the darkness and out of town laughing like the two drunks they were. The hunter's name was Ald Stacker. They camped in the hills, and Zach told him about the place he wanted to have someday.

"Whiskey farm," the hunter had nodded.

"Whiskey farm?"

The hunter smiled. "If you gotta settle down, it's the only kinda place to have."

They rode north from Fort Carson, back into the high country, and tried hunting for two years. They were a lean two winters, but they got a little out of it. Sitting on a hotel porch one spring evening, Stacker shook his head.

"Can't make the money you used to make at huntin'. When you do, it ain't worth nothin'." He frowned and looked at the mountains, white-peaked in the blackness, then looked at Zach.

They headed south the next day, worked for another year as hands, saved their money, and settled in Bitterroot. Zach took to it right away. He had what he'd always wanted. A place to belong to. But Stacker was different. Staying in one place had been rough for him. That's when his temper started getting bad along with the drinking, but Zach learned to tolerate it. He'd never gotten mad at Ald, other than one time, and it had nothing to do with his temper.

One night on the trail Stacker had settled into his blankets.

"Sometimes," he grumbled, "sometimes I think about goin' home. You ever think about that?"

Zach shook his head, "No. Never do."

Stacker sat up. "Never. Hell, everybody—"

"I don't," Zach snapped. "I don't have a home. None but this one."

"No family?"

Zach shook his head and crawled into his blankets. "Lot of work tomorrow," he said, and lay down.

There was a silence. Then Stacker said, "Well, I ain't neither." He rustled in his blankets, "Puts us in the same boat."

Cash dropped a glass, jerking Zach's eyes up.

"Sorry," he managed to smile.

Zach looked back to his whiskey.

"Ald," he said aloud, and realized he was dead. His stomach and eyes ached hollow.

"Damn," he whispered, shoving the glass away, "Goddamn," he growled, and walked back out the door.

Mitch Prentice pushed out of Sid Coffee's workroom and hurried through the front to the cool night air outside. Leaning against the hitching post, he thought he was going to vomit.

Footfalls scraped the sidewalk behind him. Then Harry Keegan put a hand on his shoulder.

"You all right, boy?"

Mitch nodded, drawing in air, then turned back around.

"Yeah," he cleared his throat. "Looks bad for him, don't it, Harry."

The U.S. marshal nodded without saying anything.

"It just don't—" Mitch shook his head. "It just don't figure—"

"I know," Keegan said.

Mitch took off his hat and ran his fingers through his blond hair, squeezing it hard, then letting go.

"You gonna stay with it, son?"

Mitch looked up and shrugged. "It's the job I always wanted."

"That ain't what I asked. You gonna bring him in?"

"There's his side—"

"Mitch—"

The deputy stared up at the U.S. marshal, "What would you do, Harry?"

Keegan hesitated, then frowned. "You know the answer to that."

Mitch nodded, "So do you, Harry. I was trained by the best." Frowning, he whispered, "You don't let personals get into it. There's a certain way of doin' things."

Leaving Keegan at the hotel, Mitch walked down to the office. He checked the back and locked it, then looked around the room he'd shared with Gabe Early.

Less than a year, but it seemed less and more at the same time, like time had gotten slowed down and speeded up at the same time.

Things would be all right, he told himself. Gabe would go to trial, and everything would be all right. They had to be.

Slipping off his coat, the boy walked to the office bunk, then hesitated.

"Good lawman don't sleep in his office," Gabe had told him. "Makes him too easy to find."

Frowning, Mitch pulled his coat back up on his shoulders. He glanced around the room again and shook his head heavily. "It's what I always wanted, Gabe," he whispered, and balling his hand into a fist, he turned quickly and left the office.

ELEVEN

After putting a pad of torn sheet on the wound, Gabe took his money from the saddlebag, slipped it into his coat pocket, and stood up.

The wound bit into him like something with razor teeth.

Trying to ignore it, he picked up the Sharps and stepped into the hall, quickly down the back stairs and through the rear door.

Pressing himself against the wall, he stood in the cover of the door for a moment, listening.

A horse rattling his gear. Women and drunks down Howell Street, laughing.

Gabe stepped into the alley. Then back again in reflex. His eyes scanned the alley. Nothing, he shook his head— then smelled the cigarette smoke again.

His eyes moved through the darkness again.

Where the hell was he?

He couldn't see a damned thing.

Drawing his pistol, Gabe stepped from the porch to the alley, avoiding the steps, and turned up the alley toward the livery.

Smelling the smoke again, he stopped. It was ahead of him. Up and around the corner of the hotel.

Gabe backed away and crossed the alley to the line of buildings along Howell Street. He leaned against a shack and examined the street.

The smell of tortillas and peppers was strong. There were a few Mexicans and cowhands on the street. Holstering his pistol, Gabe stepped into the street, turning toward the livery and staying close to the buildings. A man wandered out of a nameless bar in front of him and stood weaving in the doorway.

Gabe stepped into the alley. He walked back toward Main Street and halted. He was a hundred feet from the corral.

Drawing his Colt again, he turned toward the livery, bending low, nearly running for the fence, the pain from his wound gnawing into him. He stopped behind the Ace-High, kneeling in the mud, his breath clawing through him.

"Kick you in the ass, Harry," he sighed, and pushing himself up again he heard the horses on Main Street. A lot of them.

Bennett had made good time.

Running now, he made it to the fence and crawled through, then crouched low, his eyes on the barn. A dim light burned, and he could see the flutter of a shadow.

Gabe crawl-walked to the far end of the corral, then with the wagon between him and the door, he crouched down so he could see the door, and eased toward the caravan.

He was better than halfway to it when Dell Sumner came out of the barn.

Zach Harper waited for his men on the porch of the Holman House. They rode in, forming a horseshoe in front of him.

"Bennett," he said, "go down to the livery with Sumner; Archer, you and Tom head for the north end of town; Wells and Evans, the south; the rest of you scatter along the street. I want this town turned inside out. And one more thing: Don't kill him. Whatever you do, don't kill him."

Lying in the mud, Gabe watched Dell Sumner stroll into the yard. The cowhand ambled into the darkness, unhitched his jeans, and was relieving himself when somebody called to him.

"What?" he called, looking toward the barn.

Gabe pushed himself up and around the wagon, opening the door quietly.

Bennett ambled through the barn and into the corral.

"Boss said to look ever'thing over."

"Look ever'thing over," Sumner nodded, "sure."

"Let's get the wagon," Bennett said, "then look around the barn."

Sleeping in his wagon, Silas Toomey felt something cold on his cheek, and lifted his hand to brush it away. A voice stopped him.

"Don't move, Toomey, and don't say anything."

The preacher jerked, blinking his eyes open. The first thing he saw was the gun barrel, then in the darkness a man.

"Who's there—"

"Early—now shut up." The voice was calm, businesslike.

"Ear—"

The gun barrel pushed against his face, and Gabe pressed

closer. "A couple of men coming," he said quickly, and shifting, he crawled under the bunk. "If you try anything," he promised, "you'll never get out of this caravan alive." The lawman lay back and disappeared under the bunk, and the preacher heard the hammer snap back.

Voices outside jerked his eyes up and to the door.

"Anybody to home?" one of the voices called, and the door rattled under the impact of a fist.

"Yes, dammit," Toomey snapped.

The door jerked open and a head poked inside. A man wearing a hat, with heavy-lidded eyes.

"You alone in here?"

"No," Toomey glared, "I've got a naked girl hanging on the wall. Now what the hell do you want?"

The cowhand's eyes glanced at the wall, then back to the preacher. "Ain't no way for you to talk."

"All right," Toomey sighed, "what do you want?"

"Lookin' for a fella."

"Anybody in particular?"

"Early. Killed Stacker."

Toomey shook his head. "Well, he's not here."

Shrugging, the heavy-lidded man looked over his shoulder. "Ain't here," he said to the other man.

"He got any of that medicine oil?"

"Another head came inside. "How 'bout some of that cure-all? Ain't feelin' so good."

"Damn," Toomey growled, and getting out of bed, he fished a bottle from a box beside the door and handed it to the cowhand. The cowhand took the bottle and gave the preacher fifty cents, then was gone.

Toomey looked back at the bed. "All right," he said wearily, "they're gone."

Gabe's head came from under the bed, his eyes on the door, then he smiled ruefully. "Hidin' under a preacher's bed. Damn," he sighed, then looked up at Toomey. "You ain't gonna like this, Brother Toomey, but you and me have just become joined in purpose—"

Zach Harper walked into the livery barn as Sumner and Bennett were coming in from the corral.

"Anything?" he asked.

Bennett shook his head. "Nothin', boss."

Zach frowned tightly. "He's around here someplace. That's his horse," he pointed to the bay in his stall. "Go over this place. And if you don't find him, go over it again."

Turning, he walked back into the street and down to Spanner, Wells, and Evans at the south end of town. Wells and Evans sat on both sides of the street; Spanner stood in the middle of the street with a rifle.

"How 'bout it?" he said to Spanner.

"Town looks dead," the foreman answered him. "Nobody's come this way."

Zach nodded sourly.

"He'll move," he said, "he'll move." He looked back to his foreman. "You been at it all day, ain't you?"

"A while," Spanner nodded.

Zach frowned. "Take a turn around town, and see if anybody's turned anything. And I mean anything. I'll be up in the Holman House. And Spanner—"

"Yeah, boss?"

"Get some sleep, because if he don't turn up tonight we're gonna start all over again tomorrow."

Spanner nodded. "Thanks, boss."

Zach turned and walked up the street, his eyes moving to the shadows and alleys.

"Come on, Gabe," he whispered, "just move."

He climbed the steps of the Holman House and went upstairs.

Toomey shook his head. "It ain't gonna work, Marshal."

Gabe sat on the floor, his back against the bunk. "Has to, Toomey. Half a day south of here is McAllister's, the stage

way station. All you have to do is get me there. By then I'll
have some time. This wound should be some better, and I
can get a horse there and head for Crucero Vado and Mexico.
Ain't much of a chance, but it's a better one than I had."

Toomey was still shaking his head. "That ain't what I'm
talking about," he said. "That woman. The red-haired one.
I told her I'd take her to Hatchet."

Gabe thought for a moment. "We'll go ahead and take
her. She'd get 'em on to us if we left her."

"All right, all right," the preacher nodded, then he looked
up. "Marshal—"

"Yeah?"

"I'll help you. Do what you say, but just do one thing
for me."

"What's that, preacher?"

"Just . . ." Toomey's eyes roamed over the interior of his
wagon, "Just don't bust up my caravan, Marshal. It's all I
got."

Gabe smiled suddenly. "Now, why the hell would I do
that?"

Toomey shrugged reluctantly, "I don't know . . . hell, I
don't know. I never figured on this . . . none of it. . . ."

"Neither did I, preacher." Gabe frowned, "You better get
some sleep now—we got a long way to go tomorrow—"

TWELVE

Late in the night he heard the rain come. First light, then
heavy, and easing off again. Gabe sat for a long time listening
to it. It was a remembering sound, a childhood murmur. He

sat and thought about a lot of things, but the boy, Mitch, seemed to be more on his mind than anything else.

Toomey growled a snore, jerking Gabe's eyes around; then, smiling, the old lawman sat back against the wall and shook his head. Here a man with a gun was sitting on the floor of his—Toomey's—wagon, and Toomey was sleeping the sleep of the innocent.

"Amazing," Gabe sighed, and realized that light had breathed into the wagon. He shifted to look at his watch, and a sharp bite of pain spiked through his side. Sweat bubbled on his face like burning lace, and for a moment he couldn't breathe. He shook his head and looked at his watch. There was pain again, but he was used to it now.

"Worse'n I figured," he whispered to himself, and saw his hand trembling.

Toomey stirred in his bunk, and reaching out, Gabe touched the preacher on the shoulder with his gun barrel.

Toomey rustled and pulled his blankets up over his head.

Frowning, Gabe tapped him again—harder. "Get up, preacher," Gabe growled in a whisper.

Toomey peered up and over his blankets. "What?" he mumbled thickly.

"Get ready," Gabe said.

Zach Harper jerked awake where he'd fallen asleep fully clothed in a chair in his room. Frowning, he picked his hat off the floor and went next door and pounded on Coy Spanner's door.

A muffled voice answered.

"Get up," Zach said. Without waiting for an answer, he turned and walked downstairs. He ate a breakfast of eggs, steak, pancakes, coffee, and blueberry jam. He was nearly finished when Spanner came into the dining room.

"Mornin', boss," he said, easing his gaunt frame into a chair, yawning.

"Anything happen last night?"

Spanner shook his head. "I'd'a tole you if it had."

"I mean anything out of the ordinary?"

Spanner thought for a moment, then shook his head. "No, boss, nothin'."

Frowning, Zach drank the last of his coffee. "I'll see to the other boys. When you finish take over at the livery, and let 'em eat one at a time. On me."

"That's nice of you, boss."

"No it ain't," Zach said, standing up. "They just might get their asses shot off for me. Breakfast is a small price for gettin' your ass shot off."

Spanner smiled lightly. "Guess it is at that."

Zach turned and looked through the window to the street. "Good rain," he nodded. "Gonna be some good pasture this year." He looked back to Spanner. "I'm goin' up to the north end of town and let them come down and eat."

He left Spanner and walked into the lobby of the Holman House. There was a woman at the desk. Tall, red-haired.

"Damn," he sighed admiringly and walked out into the rain.

Toomey took money from Gabe, paid Fred Legate, then hitched the horses to the caravan.

Holding his side, Gabe watched Toomey through the doors that led to the driver's seat, then sitting down again, looked at his watch.

Damn near seven o'clock.

He took a careful look out of the doors again, and pulled his head back, frowning.

Toomey came in the back of the wagon and sat down shivering.

"Where the hell is she?" Gabe snapped.

Toomey shook his head helplessly. "I don't know, Marshal."

"Anybody out there?"

The preacher jerked his eyes up. "Anybody what?"

"Any of Harper's men."

"I don't know," the preacher shrugged. "Hell, I—"

"Take a look," Gabe ordered him.

Nodding wearily, the preacher crawled out through the back.

"And preacher—" Gabe said.

Toomey looked back inside. Gabe lit a lantern, and setting it on the floor, unholstered his gun, and cocking the hammer, leveled it at the lantern.

"Don't try anything," the old lawman said.

The preacher's head jerked in a trembling nod as he turned away, closing the door.

Gabe sat in the flickering darkness for a moment, and frowning, he rested the hammer down, laid the gun on the bed, and blew the lantern light out.

"Now you've taken to scarin' preachers," he sighed distastefully.

Toomey waded through the mud into the barn, then into the street. Holding his collar up against the rain, he saw men at both ends of town, and more with guns along the street. A bearded man came out of the Holman House and walked toward him.

Wheeling back around, the dark preacher rushed back through the barn to his wagon.

Stepping into his wagon, he was trembling. "People all over the place," his hands were shaking. "Marshal, it ain't gonna work, it just—"

"Gonna have to, preacher," Gabe nodded. "Damn," he growled, "we've gotta get out of here."

"The woman—"

"We can't wait," Gabe decided. "We stay here any longer and they'll go through this thing again. No," he shook his head, "let's go, Brother Toomey. Now."

"Leavin' us already?" the desk clerk said politely to Jenny Shannon.

"Yes," she nodded, "I'm going to Hatchet this morning." She paid her bill, and carrying her two suitcases, she walked

out onto the porch of the hotel and opened her umbrella.
Lifting the umbrella over her head, she saw Toomey drive
out of the livery and turn it toward her.

Smiling, she nodded. It was very nice of him to come for
her.

Toomey came up the street and passed her. He did not
look in her direction.

For a moment she thought he was going to come back, then
realized he was not.

"Mr. Toomey," she said softly at first, then turning down
the walk, she called to him, "Mr. Toomey."

Inside the wagon, Gabe heard the woman. He looked
through the doors to the driver's seat.

"What the hell is that?" he demanded in a whisper.

"The woman," Toomey murmured back.

"Mr. Toomey," the woman called again.

"Well, stop, goddammit." Gabe growled. "She'll have the
whole town out here in a minute."

Toomey reined the horses in and looked to the woman
on the sidewalk.

"Oh, hello, Miss Shannon."

"Mr. Toomey," she said, catching her breath, "for a moment I thought you were leaving without me."

"Oh—no, ma'am. Come on and climb aboard."

"My bags—" she gestured to the porch of the hotel.

Toomey leaned out into the rain and looked back down
the street, then turned the wagon and drove it to the front
of the Holman House.

Gabe sat down on the bed. "Sonofabitch," he muttered,
and wiped the sweat off his face.

Toomey jumped off the wagon onto the walk, picked
up the two suitcases, and shoved them on the driver's seat.

Jenny came back up the walk behind him as he was thrusting the bags through the small door into the back.

"Where were you going, Mr. Toomey?"

The preacher jerked up and looked around at the woman.

"Goin', ma'am?"

"Yes, Mr. Toomey," she repeated, "where were you going?"

"Oh," Toomey shrugged, "I was just . . . I was just goin' down the street to a little place to get some breakfast."

"I'm sorry," she said. "Are you hungry? I could—"

"No," Toomey shook his head, "I'm not hungry now, just want to get on our way."

Two cowhands rode up the street and halted in front of the hotel.

"Ma'am," Toomey said, holding out his hand, "would you like to get up here—"

"No," the woman said, "I'd like to ride in the back, what with the weather and all."

The two cowhands dismounted.

"Old Harper's sure got a fire under him," one of them said.

Toomey glanced at the cowhands, then at the woman, and paled. "In the back . . . all right, ma'am."

The two cowhands came up the steps as Toomey walked toward the back with Jenny.

"Damn," one of the cowhands growled and stopped in front of the door.

"What's wrong, Ben?" the other asked.

"Boot," Ben answered. "Think . . ." he lifted his boot, and holding it in his hand, he examined the sole. "Got a goddamn hole in it, Walt—" He looked up, "Look at that. Goddamn hole in my boot."

At the rear of the wagon, Toomey touched the latch of the door and glanced at the cowhands.

"Mr. Toomey?" Jenny said, and he looked at her.

"Seems to be stuck," he answered and jerked on the latch harshly, keeping it secured.

Down the walk, the cowhand named Ben stomped his boot down on the wood.

"Bought that boot a year ago," he shook his head. "You'd think they'd do better'n that—"

Toomey still jerked at the latch, watching the men, and smiling at Jenny.

"Old door," he offered, and looked back at Harper's men.

"Yeah," Walt said, shaking his head. "Let's get somethin' to eat," he said, and they both went inside.

For a moment, Toomey thought his bowels were going to give on him, and sighing, he opened the back.

Jenny rushed down the steps, and Toomey boosted her up into the back, through the doorway. She was turning to thank the preacher when a shadow moved beside her and something hard closed over her mouth, smothering her words back.

She jerked frantically, trying to get free.

"Miss Shannon," whispered a voice, "now calm down. There are some men trying to kill me. If I let you go, do I have your word you won't scream?"

Jenny nodded against the force of the hand.

The hand slipped away from her mouth, and she looked around. It was the marshal. Her eyes widened with a mixture of fear and anger.

"What is—"

Gabe pressed his hand to her mouth again. "Please, Miss Shannon," he said.

The wagon jerked, and Gabe could feel them turning. "We have to go by a couple of men up here, now just stay quiet until then, ma'am."

She nodded and Gabe let go of her mouth and sat her down on the bed. "Now please, ma'am," he whispered, and drew his pistol.

Jenny's eyes widened at the sight of the gun.

"Marshal—"

"I don't have time," the old lawman snapped. "Now shut up," he ordered her.

Jenny sank back on the bed. She felt the wagon slowing, then stop.

"Now be real quiet, ma'am," Gabe said in a whisper.

On the wagon seat, Toomey pulled up the horses and smiled at the man in the rain. It was the same one that had stuck his head in the wagon last night.

"Still ain't found him?" Toomey nodded.

The cowhand shook his head. "Found him? Nope," he answered. " 'Fraid not."

"You want to look again?"

The cowhand smiled. "Look again? No. You can—" he hesitated, "could use some of that tonic, though, for warmin'. Kept me and ole Flowers warm last night. Where is it back here—" he turned.

"No," Toomey almost shouted. "Here," he said, "got some right here inside the door."

He pushed the door open a crack and looked at Gabe. "It's right here someplace."

Gabe looked around. All the preacher's tonic was in a box by the back door. He reached around quickly, pulled a bottle out, and slapped it in the preacher's hand.

Toomey turned back around. "Here it is."

The preacher leaned down, and the cowhand handed him fifty cents.

The cowhand uncorked the bottle and took a draw. "Yessir," he smiled.

Toomey pocketed the fifty-cent piece. "Good luck," he said, and strapped the horses.

Inside the wagon, Gabe holstered his pistol and sat down gently next to Jenny. He glanced at her with a twinge of discomfort and shook his head.

He looked at her for a long moment, then said: "I don't suppose you play cards, do you?"

THIRTEEN

Mitch Prentice only half noticed Toomey's wagon rolling out of town. Instead his gaze followed Harper walking toward the north end of town. Harper was spelling one of his men guarding the north end of the street.

"Mornin', son," a voice said behind him, and Mitch jerked.

Harry Keegan smiled as he stepped up on the walk and under the eve of the building out of the rain.

"Mornin', Harry—" Mitch nodded.

"How was your night?" Keegan asked.

Mitch cleared his throat. "Well—"

Keegan nodded, "I didn't sleep either."

Mitch frowned and gestured in Zach's direction. "He seems to be doin' our job for us."

Keegan rubbed his nose slowly.

"There's a time for movin' and a time for not. Zach—" he shrugged. "He's a funny sort. Stacker was like, well, his family, I suppose. They were together a long time." He looked at the deputy. "You ever have somethin' hurt you so bad all you could do was hit somethin'?"

Mitch nodded vaguely.

"Zach's like that," Keegan said. "No use tryin' to stop him. Only way to do it would be to kill him. And I'm not sure I could manage it. Best we can do is run his rope. Besides," Harry said, "I like him."

"While we're sittin' around watchin' him, he's liable to get to Gabe."

"We'll have to get to him first."

Mitch shook his head skeptically. "He's got a helluva lot of men, Harry—"

Keegan shook his head. "No. When he goes after Gabe, he'll go after him alone. He's an honorable man, Mitch."

"He'll shoot Gabe down cold if he gets the chance."

Keegan watched Zach relieve the man at the far end of the street.

"I don't know," the U.S. marshal said, weighing his words. "I don't know about that, Mitch." He looked back at the deputy. "I do know I got to be there when he gets to Gabe."

"How you gonna do that?"

Keegan shook his head, then looked toward the livery. "By bein' there when he makes his move. Come on, boy, I've got a thought—"

Gabe cracked the back door of the wagon open and peered back toward town.

"Mr. Early—" Jenny probed insistently.

"Not right now, Miss Shannon."

"Mr. Early," she said standing up, "I want out of this wagon right now."

Gabe looked up at her incredulously.

"What?"

"I want out of this wagon right now," she repeated emphatically.

"Ma'am—"

"I don't know what this is all about, but I want out of this wagon this minute. I'll walk back if need be." She looked forward, "Mr. Toomey—"

"Toomey, keep this wagon movin'," Gabe commanded. He looked at Jenny. "Miss Shannon," his face hardened, "if you go back there now, I'm a dead man."

Jenny's face whitened. "Why, I—"

"Now sit down and be quiet, Miss Shannon, or I'm going

to tie you up and let you ride to McAllister's Station that way."

Jenny sat down easily again.

"There's no need for you to be worried, ma'am," Gabe said. "Any luck at all," the lawman frowned, and cracking the back door open again, he watched the trail behind them. An hour out of town the rain webbed back, shadowing the peaks of the mountains.

The wheels of the wagon slammed through a mudhole, jostling Gabe into the wall, and his hand went to his side.

"Mr. Early?" Jenny said from the bed.

"I'm all right, ma'am," he said tightly.

"Are you hurt?"

"A little," he nodded, "but it's no mind." He sat up again and watched the road behind them.

They rode for a while longer, then Jenny asked: "Are you looking for something, Marshal?"

Gabe nodded. "In a way, yes, ma'am. The man that's after me."

"But you're the marshal."

"Not anymore, ma'am."

"I don't understand."

Gabe eased his leg under him and tried to get in a better sitting position.

"Ma'am," Gabe began, and the wagon dipped into another mudhole, jerking the old lawman around, ripping pain through him. He tried to put his hand out but fell, slamming into the floor. Darkness flushed him and black sweat laced his back and face again. His breath rattled against the floor, and he could hear the woman beside him.

"Mr. Early," she was saying, then her voice was turned away. "Stop—stop now," she shouted, and Gabe pulled himself over.

"No," he managed, "no." He shoved himself up and shouted toward the door that led to the driver's seat. "Toomey?"

"What's wrong back there?" the preacher called.

"Nothin'," Gabe said. "Just keep going." Trembling, he rested back against the side of the wagon.

The woman knelt beside him. "You're hurt, Mr. Early," she said, and he could feel her careful fingers parting his shirt and then heard the catch of her breath.

"This is mud," she said disgustedly. "I'm going to clean this," she informed him with a tone that told him he had no choice in the matter.

She worked quickly and surely. She found water and clean linen. She cleaned the wound, then swabbed it out with some of Mr. Toomey's liniment. With that done, she wrapped Gabe securely with the bandages she'd torn from the linen.

Gabe watched the woman with one eye and kept another on the door and the road behind him.

Finished, Jenny smiled. "Surely they won't know that you're in this wagon. And besides, Mr. Toomey is helping you."

Gabe nodded. "Toomey'll help me as long as he has to—and Zach'll know, believe me," he set his jaw, "he'll know. He thinks the way I do."

The wagon rocked harshly, then stopped.

Gabe looked forward.

"What the hell are we doin' now?" he called to Toomey, and struggling to his feet, he went forward. He pulled the doors open and leaned outside.

Toomey nodded forward, and Gabe's eyes followed. Eight-mile Creek rushed before them, rain-swollen and stretching out of its banks.

A coldness fishhooked Gabe's stomach. It had been upstream from here that he'd killed Stacker. Frowning, he shook his head and looked at Toomey.

"Better take 'em in at a slant," Gabe said, "then—"

"I've been drivin' this wagon for six years, Marshal," Toomey said curtly.

"Just suggestin'—"

"I know what to do. Fella learns how to take care of what
he's got—"

"You're awful goddamn touchy about a suggestion."

Toomey shrugged, "Just that this damn thing's all I got."

Gabe nodded. "Have at it, then."

"Yeah," Toomey nodded and surveyed the creek again.

The creek swarmed through a stand of willow and salt
cedar, rushing the trunks of trees with water. There were
a lot of trees down in here, but a hill pulled away from the
water about twenty feet across. Toomey examined the water
itself. Small mounds of rock threaded up, and branches V'd
the water. It wasn't so much deep as it was wide.

Toomey sighed and brought the horses around, then pushed
them into the creek on a slant.

"Give 'em hellfire and whatfor," Gabe winked, then had
to grab hold as the wheels jounced over the rocks and were
hit by the water. He felt someone at his side and looked
around to see Jenny peering curiously through the doors.

In front of them Toomey's horses strained against the har-
nesses and water, inching the wagon through the water.

Toomey stood up in the seat well and strapped the horses.
Beneath them the brown water twisted like earthdreaming
clouds, and the hill beyond began to gather through the trees.

The wheels ground over a hump of rock and back into the
water again, cutting toward the rising ground. Toomey
strapped the horses, yelling at them, and they strained, tauten-
ing the leads and harness, their muscles rounding, gleaming
and hard in the wetness, carrying them forward, moving
again against the strap of leather as if it were natural.

Toomey hit them again, and the back wheels cut over a
log, then slipping, snapped and jerked to one side—and down,
landing hard. Toomey cracked the reins and the wagon
strained, wood moaning, but rocked back again, settling off
to one side.

"Hole," Toomey growled.

Gabe nodded, wordlessly went to the back, and stepped down into the knee-high water. Holding to the back step, he leaned over and could see that the right rear wheel had sunk lower than the other.

He waded around to the front of the wagon. "We need a lever," he said, and kept going to the bank. Toomey climbed down from the wagon and followed him into the trees. Gabe hesitated, his eyes combing the brush for something big enough to use as a lever.

"There," Toomey said, pointing to a good-sized piece of wood.

Gabe stepped forward, pushing through the brush, then stopped again when he saw the blood, and realized he was looking at a man's leg.

"What the—" the preacher whispered.

Drawing his pistol, Gabe walked to the body, knelt down, and turned it over.

"Jesus," Toomey gagged.

The man on the ground had been shot twice. Once in the leg. Another slug had torn through his middle.

Leaning down, Gabe examined him. The slug through his middle had been a Sharps. Gabe stood up and looked back down the creek.

"Stacker," he nodded.

"What?" Toomey said.

"Nothing," Gabe shook his head. Using his boot, he rolled the man over.

"You know him?" Toomey asked.

"Name's Hamp Clay," Gabe nodded. "Rides with a fella named Woody Sizemore. Likely it was Sizemore's boys that robbed the express office yesterday."

"Express office?"

Gabe turned back around and shook his head amazedly. "That must be damn good stuff you sell, preacher. Express office was robbed yesterday morning."

Toomey swallowed. "You mean they could be out here someplace?"

"Is something wrong?" Jenny called from behind them.

Gabe turned hurriedly and caught her as she waded from the creek. "Don't come up here—"

Coming out of the water, Jenny's eyes fixed on the dead man.

"Oh, my God—"

Gabe rushed to her turning her away from the body.

"Get back on the wagon," he ordered her.

He eyes jerked up. "I . . . I'm not a child, Mr. Early." She steadied her voice, "What's happened?"

"It's one of the men that robbed the express office yesterday mornin'—"

"The others," Toomey broke in, "you say they could still be around here?"

Gabe thought for a moment, then shook his head. "No. They're headed for Mexico. Down through Crucero Vado." He frowned. "Only place they can cross the river."

"Ain't that where you're headed?"

Gabe nodded, still frowning.

"Guess this changes that, don't it?"

Gabe's eyes hardened. "No," he said. "Don't change a damn thing. I'm still goin' south. Through Crucero Vado. It's the only way I've got."

Jenny shook her head. "I don't understand. You mean you'd go through this place knowing you might encounter those outlaws?"

"Yes, ma'am," Gabe nodded.

"That seems a little foolish, Mr. Early—"

Gabe frowned. "Not when you've been tryin' to go as long as I have. I'm goin' home, Miss Shannon. I don't give a dogleg who's in Crucero Vado, Woody Sizemore or Teddy Roosevelt. I'm goin' through. Nothin's gonna stop me."

He glanced around. "Now let's find somethin' to get the

hell out of that creek with. Zach's gonna figure out where I am before long, and I'd rather get a little more time on him."

By three o'clock Harper had finished searching the town, and found nothing. He left two men at both ends of Main Street and went into the Ace-High.

"Set 'em up for the whole bunch," he said to the barkeep, Lon, as his men filed in and leaned against the bar.

"I don't understand it," Spanner bellied up beside him. "He's got to be here someplace. We had this town bottled up."

Zach shook his head. "No, he's gone," he said. "Question is where and how."

"Nobody left town," Spanner said. He looked down to Dell Sumner. "How many went by you this mornin'?"

"By me this mornin'?" Dell repeated, and mulled a second. "Foss Adams and the preacher."

"How many by you?" the foreman asked Bennett.

Bennett shook his head. "Three miners. Ain't no day to be tryin' to go somewhere. Nobody but a fool be out on a day like this."

"Nobody but a fool—" Sumner nodded, then smiled. "Goddamn that preacher'll be havin' a helluva time with that wagon of his. Wouldn't want to be drivin' that big lumberin' sonofabitch of a thing."

Zach glared down the bar at Sumner. He was the talkin'est person he knew. Zach picked up his bottle and ambled to a table. Sumner was still talking as Zach eased back in his chair, sighing.

"How the hell'd you do it, Gabe?" he whispered to himself.

". . . what the hell would anybody want to wrestle a thing like 'at for?" Sumner was talking to Flowers now.

Zach sipped his whiskey concentrating, and something seemed to hang in his mind.

"Hell, you'd get stuck in ever' creek 'tween here and points south. . . ."

Zach lowered his glass back to the table, looking around to the bar.

". . . damn thing's big enough to put a corral in, why all—"

Zach pushed his chair back. "You look inside?"

Sumner looked back over his shoulder. "Inside?" he blinked as Zach came toward him.

"Did you look inside it?" Zach repeated harshly. "Inside the preacher's wagon?"

"Yeah," Sumner nodded, then added, "last night."

"Not today when he left town?"

Sumner shook his head. "No," he answered in a low voice, "I just figgered—"

"You figured," Zach growled, "Goddamn—"

He strode across to the door. "You people go on back to the ranch," he said back over his shoulder, pushing through the swinging doors to the outside.

Spanner followed and caught up with him in the street.

"How many of us you want, boss?"

"None," Zach answered, still walking.

"You . . . don't want none?"

"Goin' it alone," the hawk-faced rancher said.

Spanner walked with him for a moment, then fell behind, left standing in the street as Zach walked away from him and into the livery barn.

The big rancher saddled his black quickly and led him out of the stall. He only half saw the movement behind him. Dark and quick. He turned toward it, and the rifle butt smashed into his back, driving him to the ground, slamming him to his hands and knees. He tried to push himself back up, and a fist pummeled him behind the ear, crushing him back into the dirt.

His head roared and he tried to get up again, but it all seemed disconnected, floating. He put one hand down, and

it was jerked out from under him. Then the other. Both
hands were pinned behind him, and then he felt the steel
close.

Kicking air, he rolled over on his back. Harry Keegan
stood over him. Next to him was the deputy, Mitch Prentice.

"You hit me behind," Zach growled.

Harry nodded, smiling faintly. "Not too honorable," he
sighed, and the smile faded. His eyes fixed on Zach. "Where
is he?"

"I don't know."

"You were comin' for your horse, Zach. Alone. Where is
he?"

"Go to hell."

Keegan shrugged. "All right, Zach. You can sit in jail a
couple of days and Gabe can get clean away."

The bearded man pulled in a deep breath. "You'll do that
anyway."

Keegan shook his head. "No, your boys'd just bust you out
and I'd have to handle all of you." He knelt down. "I'll
make a deal with you, Zach. I'll take you along."

Zach fought against the cuffs again, then rested back in the
dirt.

"At least he ends up in jail this way," Harry nodded, "and
maybe dead. You've always got that chance."

Zach stared at the ground.

"What's it gonna be?" Keegan asked.

Zach nodded harshly.

"Your word on it."

The bearded man's eyes jerked up.

"Your word, Zach."

There was no defeat in his eyes as he nodded. "All right."

"Say it," Keegan insisted.

The muscles gathered through the beard. "You sonofabitch," he whispered. "I said you have my word and you
have it."

Nodding, Keegan took the keys to the cuffs from his pocket and unlocked the steel.

The bearded man pulled himself out of the straw and mud and walked to his horse.

"Damn," Harry sighed, "more time on horseback—"

"I'll get 'em," Mitch said.

"Just mine," Harry said, turning to the boy.

Mitch stared back at him. "I'm goin'—"

The U.S. marshal shook his head sternly. "No, boy, you're not."

"Harry—"

"Do it," Keegan said, a final tone hardening his voice.

Nodding listlessly, the deputy turned away. Watching him, Harry frowned. He hadn't liked doing that. He liked the boy and knew why he wanted to come along. But more than liking the boy, he remembered Gabe back there in the afternoon talking about dead men. Gabe was his friend. He couldn't do much for him anymore, except maybe keeping Mitch from becoming one of them.

Mitch watched Keegan and Harper ride out of town, then frowning deeply, he went back to the office. He walked aimlessly across the room and ended up slumped behind his desk.

"Damn . . ." he grumbled, "damn."

Lifting his boots, he propped them on his desk. He sat staring at them for a long time. Gabe had bought him those boots after he'd shot himself in the toe practicing his fast draw. A pair of boots for being clumsy. Like a kid. And now like a kid he'd been told to stay home and be a good boy.

He stood up and walked to the window. He was supposed to be the law here now. A lawman like he'd always wanted to be. A lawman made to sit home like a snot-nosed kid. Like the kid Gabe had given the boots to. Frowning, he turned to the rifles on the wall. He was going to finally earn those boots. Taking a rifle down, he locked the door and walked to the livery.

FOURTEEN

The wagon rolled through another creek, and Toomey peered at the sky. The clouds seemed to have slipped back some now.

"Might just make it if I push it a little tonight," the preacher said more to himself than to Gabe, sitting next to him on the wagon seat.

"Could be," Gabe nodded.

Toomey blinked and looked at him with dark, wet eyes as if Gabe had intruded on him.

"Figger it'll be a good town?" Gabe asked, "For preachin', I mean."

Toomey shrugged. "New place is always good. Hell," he sighed, "in a week I can make fifty, maybe a hundred dollars. Enough to keep movin'—"

"Where to?"

Toomey stared at him blankly. "Wherever it is I'm goin' next," the preacher said, as if Gabe were stupid.

"Well," Gabe started to say, and the wheel dropped into another mudhole. Both men were jostled on the seat, and Gabe held his side. Toomey looked over the side to check the wheel.

Watches this thing like a baby, Gabe thought, and straightened himself in the seat.

"Want me to spell you awhile?" Gabe offered.

Toomey shook his head.

"No," he said, "I'll do the drivin'. My wagon."

Shaking his head, Gabe looked out in front of them. The

mountains stretched down into rimrock country. High ridges
and mesas with century-brown bones cutting through, lying
twisted out, runneling like great animals that had been stilled
in motion and rivers that had forgotten the direction to the
sea. They reached until the sky blurred them.

Gabe noticed that the preacher was using the brake a bit
more now, and realized they were headed down Long's Canyon, coming off a high plateau, using a road the stage line
had blasted out of the side of it and reinforced the road with
gravel and dirt. They had done it to save five hours between
Bitterroot and Hatchet, but Gabe had always thought it was
a helluva place to put a road. On one side there was sheer
rock; on the other, a two-hundred-foot drop into a canyon.

Toomey touched the brake again, bouncing through a
rain-washed bare spot. He jerked the reins to keep the horses
in rhythm with the wagon.

Gabe eased back but felt an edge of restlessness. He
glanced back at Jenny. She sat on Toomey's bed, her back
against the wall, her head tilted in sleep. Gabe smiled softly.
She needed it. What a helluva thing to happen to her. Shaking
his head, Gabe turned back around and surveyed the country.
The longer he sat, the more he found himself thinking about
Mitch, and he frowned at that.

The boy was behind him now. On his own. Maybe even
on his trail. If Mitch was acting the way a lawman should, as
Gabe thought he would, then the young deputy was certainly on his trail.

He knew Zach would be. And Harry. Keegan didn't let
personals get in the way of things. That was the way it had
to be. And that was the way Gabe had taught Mitch.

There were three after him for certain.

Maybe more.

He would just have to find a way to outrun them.

The wagon slammed through another rut, and Gabe's eyes
jerked up.

"Damn rain," Toomey growled, and Gabe saw what he

was talking about. In the places the road had been reinforced with dirt and gravel, the rain had begun to chew it away.

"Take it easy," he warned the preacher.

Toomey didn't answer, but kept his eyes on the horses and the trail, his hands taut in the leather stringing back from the horses.

They were going down now, crawling along the ledge of rock.

Suddenly it seemed like there was nothing between them and the two-hundred-foot drop but very narrow road. Gabe tried not to pay any attention to what was going on, but couldn't. He could feel the wheels of the wagon slip every now and then, and Toomey's long, thin arms would adjust the horses, speaking to them with the leather. Sunlight glinted off ripples of sweat on the preacher's forehead.

"Toomey?" Gabe said questioningly.

"I'm doin' fine," he said.

The wagon twisted beneath them, and Toomey pistoned his arms.

Gabe looked down at the road. It still seemed all right. Just a lot of bumps and holes. He took a quick look at the woman and saw her looking at him, worry heavy in her face. Smiling, he said, "It'll be fine, ma'am, just—"

They twisted violently, slamming Gabe into the preacher. By the time he was sitting up again, Toomey had the caravan stopped, his eyes fixed ahead of them. Gabe followed his gaze, and saw what the preacher was looking at. About ten feet down the road, about six feet of ground was a good six inches lower than the rest of it.

"Stage got over it," Toomey growled.

"Two days ago," Gabe nodded. "Maybe. If they came this way. Besides, we've had a helluva lot of rain since then."

"Ain't no other way," Toomey said.

"We can take the horses and leave the wagon—"

The preacher's eyes snapped to Gabe's. "No," he said, "ain't leavin' the wagon."

"Then turn this thing around. We might make it down the old trail. Better chance'n here."

Toomey shook his head. "We'd never make it to Hatchet that way. Not tonight."

"Goddammit," Gabe said tightly, "you're not goin' to make it at all—"

"It's my wagon," Toomey hissed. "I'm a free man and I'm gonna stay this way. Now you and the woman get off. I'm takin' this wagon down."

Gabe started to say something more and saw it was useless. He looked back at Jenny.

"We're gonna have to get out for a minute," he said, and crawled through to the back. He picked up the Sharps and bandoleer and helped Jenny down the back steps to the muddy ground.

"Clear," he shouted to Toomey.

The caravan inched away from them, rocking down the road, rolling carefully onto the sunken area. For a second there, Gabe thought it was going to make it. Then the ground dropped another foot under the wagon, as if somebody had jerked out a stop beneath it.

"Stay here," Gabe said to Jenny, and was running down the slope. He went between the wagon and the rise and around to the front. Toomey was sitting in the seat hunched over and shivering.

"Don't move it," Gabe said quietly.

Toomey nodded.

"We can take the horses off. Maybe it'll sit for a while . . . you can come back for it . . ."

Toomey looked toward Gabe and started to shake his head. Gabe didn't let him say anything; instead he began unhitching the horse nearest him.

"Get down," he ordered the preacher.

Toomey's hands tightened in the leather.

"Don't pull those reins or we'll all go off this mountain," Gabe said. "Now get down."

Frowning, Toomey looked down at the precipice beside him, then nodding surrender, he climbed down.

"Dammit," Gabe said softly, "it'll be here—"

Toomey looked back at the wagon hopelessly and turned, walking up the trail. Gabe placed the rifle and cartridge belt on a rock and moved to the horses. He unstrapped the collar on the right animal, the big gray, and moved back to the single tree. He looked at Toomey, who was standing down-trail staring off into the distance. Jenny walked from behind the wagon.

"Is something wrong?" she asked.

"Better see to him," Gabe said, and unhitched the wagon's single tree.

Jenny walked down the trail, and Gabe was crossing over to unhitch the second horse, a dun-colored animal, and he heard two screams at the same time. One was the woman; the other was Toomey, charging back up the trail at him.

Gabe careened through straps and wood, his side exploding pain through him. Rolling in the mud, he saw the dun above him backing frantically. Toomey reached for him trying to hold him, getting his hand in the collar, hauling it. Gabe pushed up to his knees, whacking the free horse; then, trying to stand, he fumbled to get hold of Toomey. The preacher reeled, ramming his fist into Gabe's face, throwing him back to the ground.

Gabe hammered into the mud, his wound pulsing again, and rolling over, he tried to see against the blur of pain. Toomey was doing something. He was holding the dun, his hand still wrapped in the collar both of them seemed to be rushing backward; the wagon trembled—once, then again . . .

There was an odd, quiet roar, mixed with the ragged lash of screaming . . .

And then they were gone. Toomey, the dun, and the wagon.

The wind moved over the rocks, and the quiet seemed to explode.

Gabe sat up. Where there had been a wagon, a man, and a horse before, now there was only a space of crumbling ground.

Down the trail the woman was crying. Holding his side, shivering, Gabe heard her clearly.

FIFTEEN

Five miles south of Bitterroot, Zach Harper drew his horse in and sat for a moment. Harry reined in beside him, and both sat silent.

Zach hadn't spoken to the marshal since he had taken the cuffs off him in the barn. The bearded man looked down the stage road, and then off it into the pine and mesquite.

Then, just as abruptly as he'd stopped, Zach turned his horse off the road, threading his way through the brush.

Harry followed, shaking his head.

"You don't have to talk to me, Zach," he called to the bearded man, "but it sure is a long way to Crucero Vado."

Zach's eyes snapped back to the lawman, and then he nodded a slight but stiff acknowledgment. "You got it figured, have you?"

Harry shrugged. "We're headed south. Only place to cross the Rio Caballo is Crucero Vado. Besides, Gabe's got him a place all staked out down there. What I want to know is how you know he's gone, and why we're roamin' the tulies?"

"All right," Zach reined in his horse. "He got out of town this mornin' in the preacher's wagon—"

Keegan blurted a laugh, "Preacher's . . . oh, damn, Gabe—" He shook his head, "How do you figure that?"

"I've been through every crack in that town—"

"I'll give you that."

"Only way he could have gotten out is in the preacher's wagon." He frowned. "It was the only thing got by un-searched."

"Gabe in a preacher's wagon," Harry sighed.

"Just listen," Zach snapped. "He'll be needin' a horse—"

"McAllister's," Harry filled in for him.

"Do you want to hear this or not?"

Harry nodded.

"Usually takes seven or eight hours to get to McAllister's Station by the stage road," Zach went on, "quicker down through this way by two, three hours."

Zach looked back and up at the sky. Clouds lingered in the trees, muting the mountains, night in them somewhere.

"All that rain," Zach nodded, "might have slowed him. That two or three hours might do us some good." He shook his head. "Gonna rain again. Looks like it's gonna come an early dark too. We'd better find us a place to camp." Then turning, he looked back at Keegan. "Go back, Harry," he said without anger.

Keegan shook his head. "Gabe deserves his chance—"

Zach's mouth hardened. "Ald never had one."

"It might have been like he said, Zach. That he didn't have no time . . . it was a reflex . . ."

"You've always got a choice about killing a man, Harry. He's a killer. You and I both know it." He shifted in the saddle. "Go on home."

Keegan shook his head.

"I'll kill you if I have to."

"If you can," Harry nodded, and nudged his horse out.

The two men followed a twisting ridge through the pine. Looking back, Harry could see rain clouds filling the sky north of them, darkening the country they had just ridden, rushing to catch them. He was turning back around in the saddle when he caught a flicker of movement in the trees. Hesitating, he strained to see; then giving up, he wagged his head.

"Somethin' wrong?" Zach asked.

"No." Harry faced front, stretching his legs. "Damn horse—"

They rode on down the ridge and out of the pines. Rain began to sprinkle down on them. About a mile away Harry could see the sheer face of a mesa thrusting up before them. They rode the short distance to the face of the cliff and dismounted beside two willows. Both men worked without words. They took ponchos from their saddlerolls and tied two corners of them together with leather thongs. Then spreading the ponchos, they tied two corners between the willows, pulled the ponchos back at a slant, and tied the bottom ends to smaller brush.

Crawling under the poncho, Keegan's eye caught a shadow of movement in the trees. Frowning and shaking his head, he pulled himself under the makeshift lean-to.

"Gettin' spooky," he grumbled.

In the trees a half mile behind Zach and Keegan, Mitch Prentice rigged his poncho and sat beneath it. He didn't quite know how he was going to go about all this yet. He just knew he was, and that was that. Looking up at the rain, he sighed, frowning. They sure could have picked better weather to do it in.

"Damn," he grumbled, and sat back against a tree trunk. Above him the twilight brushed through the trees.

Riding, Gabe wanted to push the gray out, run him hard, run him until he couldn't run anymore. But he couldn't do that. The pain in his side throbbed in dull unison with the movement of the gray, and the pain fluttered against a coldness in him. His hand tightened on the Sharps he carried across his lap. He could feel them back there. Closing on him.

He glanced back at the woman riding behind him. She still looked a little stunned. After Toomey had gone over the cliff all she could do for a long time was stare at the spot where he'd been, touching a cameo that hung around her neck.

Gabe looked forward. He would leave her with McAllister and his boy, and that would be that. Maybe an hour away now. Maybe a little more.

Damn, he wanted to run that gray.

The gray moved beneath him. Steady, rhythmically, hardly varying.

Jenny Shannon held with one arm around the marshal, and felt herself moving. Toward the horizon. Behind this man who smelled of leather and tobacco. Riding. The country shifted around her, rising and falling, varying in shades of brown and green, stretching out before her, cradling the sky. It was almost as if she could see the edge of the world there in the distance. She trembled slightly behind the lawman, and his eyes came back around to her.

"Somethin' wrong, ma'am?"

"No . . ." she replied slowly, "it's just so large. . . ."

"Yes, ma'am."

"I suppose you're used to it by now."

"Sometimes," he nodded, "sometimes not. Was a time I felt at home out here. Not too much anymore."

"Used to town, I imagine."

Gabe shook his head. "No, ma'am, not really."

The gray rolled under them. The ground slipped beneath them. A line of black clouds traced the horizon. The gray moved, and Jenny felt herself wanting to sleep. But when her eyes closed she could see the empty spot where Toomey and the wagon had been.

Her eyes snapped open. Gabe was looking at her again. "You were shaking somethin' terrible," he said.

She shook her head. "Why did he do it, Mr. Early?"

"Who? Toomey?" He shrugged with his mouth. "I don't know, ma'am." He smiled gently. "What you figure on doin', ma'am?" He turned the gray up a long hill.

"What?"

"I mean, what do you figure to end up doin'? You know what I mean. Gettin' married, like that?"

"No . . ." she answered slowly, "not that."

"Why not?"

"That's a private matter, Mr. Early."

Gabe shrugged and faced forward.

Jenny stared at the back of his head. "I want to teach," she said suddenly, "to go where I want to go. I've been in school most of my life, and now I'd just like to travel."

"School. You mean college and like that?"

"Yes, and a convent for a while," she said before she thought.

Gabe stopped the horse and looked back around at her.

"A convent?" He smiled. "You were going to be a nun?"

She felt herself flush. "What's so funny about that?"

Gabe shook his head, nudging the gray out again. "Nothing, ma'am. You just sure don't look like no nun."

"Well . . ." she frowned, not knowing what to say.

"How come you didn't?" he asked.

"Didn't what?"

"Be a nun."

"Oh," she shrugged, "I . . . don't know. Perhaps I just wasn't meant to be a nun, I don't know. I decided to teach instead."

"You like it?"

"Yes."

"What do you teach? Numbers and books and like that?"

"Yes."

Gabe nodded. "I guess bein' married would kind of get in the way of travelin' and the like."

"Yes," she said, "yes, it would—"

Her voice broke off as they topped the hill, and she saw what looked like a mountain or cliff. It took a moment to realize it was a storm rushing toward them, shifting deep blue, then black, whorling spirals of water that seemed to be in continual movement, falling and rising at the same time.

"Damn," Gabe whispered.

"Shouldn't we stop, Mr. Early?" she asked, shouting against the wind.

"Can't, ma'am," was his only reply and he eased the gray out and over the ridge. The storm exploded down on them, engulfing them in water. It didn't fall in drops, but in waves, hurling down. The sudden weight of it pushed her down, then chilled her.

Huddling against the man in front of her, she could see black twists, great runnels of clouds screaming over them. She held him tighter, and without thinking, put her arm around him, against his wound, and felt him jerk.

"One arm!" he shouted, and remembering his side, she knotted the fingers of her right hand into his belt loops and tightened her arm around his side.

She thought she heard him say, "Thank you, ma'am," but wasn't sure.

Against her arm she could feel him tensing into the rain, leaning into it. Hugging her face tight into his back, she could smell him. Sweat and leather and tobacco and a sharp smell she did not know. Below her, the horse seemed to miss a step and falter. The man's muscles tensed, and she felt him wince.

Gabe couldn't see a goddamn thing.

He kept his face down, his hat brim in front of him, but the water was still swarming at his face. The gray kept moving.

"Damn," Gabe swore to himself. The rain would have to hit in broken country, not on a flat. He lifted his eyes, trying to see into the thick water-blackness. The hill was a shadow drifting away from him, sinking away into the water. Always thought rain was a good thing till now, he sighed, and nudged the gray, turning his head a little to the right. The gray stumbled and Gabe eased back on the leather as the jerk hammered through his side.

"No need for that," he growled, trembling against the pain. He had to stop; he knew that now. If he fell he'd open the wound, and if that happened he'd never make it to Mexico.

"Damn, Harry," he whispered regretfully, and the words were lost in the roar of water. Darkness and light fluttered around him like somebody shifting a kaleidoscope; then the rain came heavier.

Gabe looked up. They moved down an arroyo, which was filling up fast. Beyond that he couldn't see anything. "Goddammit," he whispered.

He was about to turn the horse back toward the ridge when he saw a dark hulk in the rain. Down the arroyo. A bluff it looked like. He turned the gray down along the water and rode under the bluff. It was tall enough for him to sit a horse under, and it kept the rain off. He eased down off the animal, then helped Jenny down. Holding the reins of the gray, he moved farther back under the bluff and sat down. Jenny stood above him, shivering.

"Sit down," he said.

She blinked, wiping water from her face. "What?"

"Sit down, Miss Shannon," he said. "You'll feel better."

Jenny smiled half-heartedly. "After being on that—horse, I . . ." her hand fluttered at the curve of her buttocks.

Gabe smiled. "Sit down, Miss Shannon. Your . . . well, you're gonna be pained for a while. Sit down and you might warm up some."

She nodded and joined him without enthusiasm. She lowered herself carefully, then sitting, she appeared as if she'd just walked in from the front porch with a glass of lemonade.

Gabe smiled. She was wet clear through. When he'd met

her going on two days ago, he would have bet she would have been crying at this point. Instead, she looked like she'd just come in from the front porch. And no complaining.

Gabe shook his head. Sometimes you just can't tell about folks.

He rested back, trying to get comfortable against a rock at the back of the bluff, but his side kept him from it.

"Why did he do it?" Jenny said again, her voice quiet, a part of the rain.

"Ma'am—"

"I'm sorry," she shrugged self-consciously, as if she'd just realized she'd spoken. "I can't seem to get Mr. Toomey out of my mind." Her eyes trembled. "I've seen a man die, Mr. Early," she whispered. "It just seems so useless."

"Most of the time it is," Gabe said, his voice clipped.

"Dying should be for something, it . . ." she shook her head, losing the words.

Gabe didn't answer her this time. The horse shifted, and the sound of the rain mingled between them. Jenny pushed her wet hair back from her face, her eyes touching on Gabe's face, then falling away. He knew the question before she asked it.

"What happened?" she finally asked, hesitantly. "Back in town, I mean."

Gabe shook his head. "Don't matter."

Jenny frowned. "Mr. Early," she said brittlely, "there's not much else to do . . . and besides," she smiled suddenly, "I don't have my cards."

Gabe tried to smile too, but shook his head wearily, "Those people back there are after me because I killed a man."

"Why?"

Gabe shifted a little to get his side in a better position. "Ma'am," he frowned, "I don't understand it myself. None of it should have happened. . . . I . . . don't know how it did. . . ." His eyes drifted to hers, and he told her about Stacker. It sounded detached when he said the words. Like it had happened to someone else. The words left something out, robbing Gabe and the men he'd killed.

"Was gonna quit," he sighed. "Headed for Mexico to buy a place of my own." He smiled ruefully, "Shoulda left a long time ago."

"Why didn't you?"

Gabe shook his head puzzledly. "Don't know, ma'am. It all got kind of fouled up."

"Fouled up?"

Gabe looked at her. "I . . . made a mistake. My deputy—"

"The young one?"

"Yes, ma'am," he nodded, "Mitch Prentice. Kind of a funny kid. Wants to be a lawman, but he'll never make it. Against his grain, if you follow me."

"I'm sorry," she admitted, smiling, "I don't."

Gabe frowned, "To be a lawman, ma'am, you have . . ." he hesitated, "you have to be able to kill people." The woman's face froze slightly. "The boy's not a killer," Gabe went on, "he's tryin' to force himself. Two–three months back he was practicin' his quick draw and he shot himself through the toe, just nicked it. Funny thing about it was, he was dry-eyed through the whole thing. Been me, I'da screamed like a wounded elk—"

"Dry-eyed?" Jenny interrupted.

"No tears, ma'am. Forced himself not to cry." Gabe shook his head. "I've seen that kind of thing before. It will finally kill him. . . ." He settled back against the rock.

The woman watched him and started to say something, but didn't. They sat silently for a long while. The rain sealed them away from the world, cocooning them, wrapping them with gray, blind rain, and a sound like yesterday.

"You're very fond of him, aren't you, Mr. Early," she said after a long time.

He looked at her, then moved his eyes back to watch the rain. He did not answer her. But then, she hadn't expected him to.

SIXTEEN

Silence awoke him. Gabe's eyes hammered open, his breath coming quick. He had been dreaming. He didn't remember about what exactly. About going back someplace he'd been before, but they hadn't known his name. Something like that. He shook his head.

The rain had stopped and left darkness behind.

He looked at the woman beside him and smiled. She was sleeping. Curled up like a child next to him, her eyes squeezed together as if she were trying to keep the darkness away.

He touched her arm and felt the tautness in her muscles.

"Ma'am," he whispered.

She exploded awake, lashing at his arms. Gabe caught her wrists and held them.

"Ma'am!" he shouted at her. "Ma'am!"

Trembling, her eyes blinked, and she seemed to see him for the first time.

"You all right, ma'am?"

"Yes," she whispered. "Yes, I'm . . . fine."

He let go of her wrists and stood up stiffly. "You sure you're all right?"

"Yes," she said again.

He nodded and turned. "Rain's stopped," he said. "Time to be movin' again."

Riding again, they moved over the dark ground. Gabe, and Jenny behind. Jenny watched giant shapes pass. Great pieces

of darkness, yet so empty. It was the emptiness that fright-
ened her.

Gabe looked back at her. "You all right, ma'am?"

"Yes," she nodded, then added slowly, "I'm sorry about
coming awake like that. I hope I didn't hurt you."

Gabe smiled. "No, ma'am. Some folks just don't like waking
up as much as others."

"Yes," Jenny said, "I guess that's it." *10298*

Jenny tried to remember what she was dreaming. But she
couldn't. She never could. Instead she held to the man in
front of her and leaned her cheek against his back. It was wet,
but comfortable . . . and strangely comforting. She was very
conscious of him, and his size. He was a hard man, quiet, and
something else. A gentleness, she supposed, something like
that. Something in his voice when he spoke of the boy,
Mitch, that she had never heard in a man's voice before. Then
frowning, she remembered the only men she had to judge
from were Stephen and her father. They were proper, and
believed in things being done in a proper order.

She remembered them giving her things, like the cameo
around her neck. And speaking to her in a passive way. About
the weather. Or the concert. Haydn was ordered, Schumann
was much too wild. Then asking her for tea.

Gabe Early had been the first man to talk to her as if she
had ears to listen.

Leaning against his back, she remembered, but mostly she
remembered his voice as he spoke of his deputy.

"Something's wrong," Gabe said, reining in the horse suddenly.

Jenny blinked and looked up. They were on a rise, and
Gabe was looking down into a small valley.

"Did you say something, Mr. Early?"

"Somethin's wrong," he said again, his voice edged.

Jenny's eyes roamed the landscape. She could see nothing.
"I don't understand, Mr.—"

"McAllister usually has a light on. His place is down there in the flat of the valley. Usually keeps a lantern goin' by his front door in case the stage is late."

"Maybe the rain—" Jenny ventured.

"Maybe," Gabe nodded. "But ma'am—"

"Yes—"

"If I say to get off this animal, you damn well get off quick."

She nodded. "All right, Mr. Early."

Gabe checked his pistol and the Sharps, then nudged the gray down the hill.

The shape of the house and barn formed slowly. Darkness within darkness. The closer they rode to the house the more Gabe noticed a couple of other things. There was no smoke smell in the air and no movement of horses from the corral.

Gabe guided the gray between the house and the barn. He reined the gray, glancing over the yard, then at the corral.

"McAllister!" he called, and felt Jenny jerk behind him. The gray must have felt it too; he switched his feet nervously, and Gabe had to steady him.

"McAllister!" he called again. A slight wind rustled in the barn. Gabe called out a third time, but there was still no answer.

Gabe eased himself down from the gray, his side biting into his bowels.

"Are you all right, Mr. Early?"

He nodded, "Yes, ma'am. I think it's healin' just fine." He handed the Sharps back up to her. "Anything happens. Anything that even sounds like trouble. You ride—"

"All right," she nodded.

Gabe walked to the house. Stepping up on the porch, glass crunched under his boots. He looked up, squinting. The lantern hanging on the peg above the door was shattered. Bringing his eyes back down, Gabe drew his pistol, and standing to one side, he eased the door open, listening for the sound of boots or breathing. After what seemed like a full minute, Gabe eased his own breath out and stepped into the house.

The room was quiet and dark. A stove to his right. Wood box. Table in the center. Two chairs and a wooden bench. Worktable with a bucket on it against the wall to Gabe's left. Door at the far end.

Gabe crossed the room and opened the door. Bed, washstand, dresser.

Gabe turned, his eyes combing the room again. The rifle rack had been above the worktable, as he remembered. He crossed to it and squinted to see in the dark. The rack was empty.

Gabe walked back outside. Jenny was still on the gray.

"Might as well get down, Miss Shannon," Gabe sighed. He walked over to the horse and gave her a hand. They went into the house, and Gabe found a lantern and lit it.

"Where are the McAllisters?" Jenny asked.

Gabe frowned. He didn't like having to tell her. "Most likely dead."

She stared at him. "Dead? Why . . . I don't . . . ."

Gabe shook his head. "Remember that man back at the creek?"

She nodded.

"The rest of that gang came through here. Likely needed horses. Maybe food. Maybe they just did it for the hell of it."

"My God," she whispered. "Why?"

Gabe shrugged heavily, "Sometimes the answer ain't as simple as the question, ma'am. One thing's for sure, though. Woody's headed for Crucero Vado, all right."

"Will you be all right?"

Gabe rubbed his nose. "If I go through quiet. Not make no trouble for 'em. Besides, like I said, I ain't got no choice."

"You could always go someplace else."

Gabe shook his head, "No," he answered determinedly, "I'm goin' home."

"You're a stubborn man, Mr. Early."

"I've been told that," he nodded. He gestured to her clothing. "You'd . . . better get out of those, ma'am. Ought to be somethin' you can wear. McAllister's boy was about your size." He looked around. "You'll do all right here, ma'am. Somebody'll be along soon. Hatchet ain't but twelve, fifteen miles."

"You'll be leaving in the morning then?"

"Yes, ma'am," Gabe nodded. "Like I said, you'll do just fine. Get to Hatchet in no time at all."

"Of course," she nodded curtly, and walked into the next room.

Shrugging, he walked back out to the gray. You'd think she'd been a bit more happy about it, he thought. She was clear of the trouble now. On her way to where she wanted to go.

"Women," he grumbled, taking the gray's reins. He took the horse into the barn, put him into a stall, unsaddled him, and then walked back to the house.

He was opening the door when he thought to call out.

"Miss Shannon—"

"Stay out," was the immediate response.

Nodding, Gabe sat down on the porch, wincing a little at his side. It was getting better. Maybe healed some. At any rate, it wasn't so bad he couldn't ride. He looked back north. Zach and Harry and the boy were after him now. He knew it. Knew it as sure as breathing. Six hours, that was about all he had on them. Six hours. At the outside.

He thought about riding on in the dark, then shook his head. Too good a chance of the horse misstepping or falling and opening his wound. If that happened he'd be done for.

"Mr. Early—"

He looked back at the door.

"Yes, ma'am?"

"You can come in now."

Gabe stretched stiffly to his feet, and turning, stepped inside. Jenny was coming through the door at the other end into the lantern's soft light. Her hair was down, falling to her shoulders, and she wore a pair of trousers and a shirt. They didn't make her any less female. Nothing could do that, he knew, except that look she got in her eyes sometimes.

He had to think to speak, then think of something to say.

"Looks . . . fine," he managed.

She smiled with embarrassment. "I . . . I've never had a man's clothes on before. I feel . . ." she shrugged the words.

"You look just fine, Miss Shannon," he reassured her. "Think I'll borrow some clothes, too. How about you makin' us some food."

Gabe went into the bedroom and found a pair of pants, shirt, socks, and a coat. With his clothes off, Gabe examined the wound in his side. It was healing. Miss Shannon had done a good job of bandaging it. He dressed and strapped his gun back on, then took the envelope with his money in it from his coat. He held it for a moment, staring at it.

Five thousand dollars. Maybe it was enough. Enough to buy him that place. . . .

He stuffed the money in his new coat and took his knife and tobacco from his old vest.

He placed the silver-handled pocket knife in the coat, then looked at what was left of the plug of tobacco. Not much, he sighed, just about a good chew. He would save it for now, he nodded. He might just need it tomorrow. Crucero Vado was a good day's ride away.

Placing the plug in his coat, he went back through the door.

SEVENTEEN

Jenny Shannon twisted in her blankets, dreaming of knives.
Lancing into her abdomen. Craving, turning, spinning her
flesh into smiling ridges, whispering faces . . . Stephen's face
. . . asking . . . and her father . . . their tongues becoming
knives . . . narrow ones with fine blades saying I love you,
I love you, I love you . . . chanting into a rhyme of edges
glinting. . . . Hands pulled her, calling through the chanting,
deadly too . . . trying to steal her, trying to . . . She felt
herself hitting, fighting against the hopeless patterning around
her. . . .
  She ripped awake. Fists beating against Gabe's chest and
face, screaming. And his hands closed around her wrists, forcing her back.
  "No, damn you," she raged, "let me loose, let me—"
  Gabe held her hands back into the pillow, forcing his chest
across hers, pinning her back into the softness. "Ma'am," he
yelled at her. "Goddammit, Jenny Shannon, lay quiet."
  "Let go of me," she screamed, then trembling, whispered,
"just . . . let go . . . of me, I'm all right. Just let go of me."
  Gabe eased his hands away from hers, and she lay in the
sheets, her breathing ragged, eyes away from his.
  She could feel him more than anything else, even though
he was no longer touching her. A form, breathing a little hard,
the smell of him very strong.
  "You gonna be all right?" he asked gently.
  She didn't answer.

"Ma'am?"

"Yes," she answered stiffly, "I just had a bad dream."

"Seems to be a habit," he said.

"No matter," she said, her hand touching her bodice, then her neck. Then groping at her throat, she sat up. "My cameo," she said, "Where is it? I know—" Her voice trembled and her eyes jerked frantically over the bed, "I had it, I know—"

Gabe crossed the room and lit a lantern. The half light seemed to blur her motions as she tore through the bedclothes. On the floor next to the bed Gabe saw the small, round object. He walked over, and picking up her cameo, he handed it to her.

"Musta come loose," he said, and she gathered it slowly from his hand.

Gabe stood for a minute. "What's the trouble, ma'am?" he asked.

She looked up. "What do you mean?"

He shook his head. "It won't work, you know."

Her eyes hardened. "What?"

"Runnin'."

Her eyes flashed. "I'm a law-abiding citizen, Mr. Early, I—"

"And a runner all the same," he said patiently. "I know the look. I know the eyes."

She looked away from him, forcing the anger out of her voice. "I'm sorry I woke you, Mr. Early. I—"

"What's back there, Miss Shannon?"

She sat quietly, turning the cameo in her hand. "No one really. My father. A man I was supposed to marry." She frowned. "A man my father told me to marry." Her eyes came up wetly.

"I . . . didn't love him, Mr. Early, so I left." She shook her head. "I don't know. I guess I just want to be free. Free to make my own choices." Her hand tightened around the cameo. "I've made one choice."

Gabe shook his head. "No, ma'am, I don't think you have. Runnin' was no choice. Stayin' would have been. Sayin' no

to them. You ain't made a choice yet to *do* somethin', only
not to do somethin'. There's the difference."

She smiled. "You talk a good game, Mr. Early. But I notice
you're running too."

"Yes, ma'am," he said quietly, "yes, I am. Stayin' would
have meant killin' more people I like. And besides that, I'm
headed *to* someplace, not away from it."

Holding the cameo in her hand, she nodded.

He put his hand out and brushed a loose strand of amber
hair back over her shoulder. "Best get some sleep now," he
said. "You need it."

He turned to the lantern and blew it out. Then looked back
at her. She made a warm sound in the sheets.

"Goodnight, Mr. Early," she said.

"Goodnight, Miss Shannon," he said, and closed the door
behind him.

Gabe crossed the room and looked down at the pallet made
for him on the floor, sighing. He was leaning down to it when
he heard the sound. It wasn't much of a sound, and for a
moment he couldn't place it. He stood back up, walked to the
door, and opened it carefully. The sound laced the wind
again. This time he knew it. A horse nickering.

Gabe turned from the door and rushed back to his bed. He
pulled his gun from its holster and cocking it, he crossed to
the door. Opening it, he slipped outside and walked barefoot
across the yard to the barn door.

The old lawman eased up to the door, listening. A scrape of
boots and hooves. Quiet. The boots were hurried. Gabe
wedged the door open. The false darkness clotted in his eyes
as he edged in and down. Waiting. He couldn't see a goddamn
thing.

A wide aisle cut down the middle of the barn, stalls on both
sides, he remembered that much. The gray was to his right,
about halfway down.

Crouching, Gabe slipped to his right, and as he did he could see movement. The gray. And somebody in the stall with him. With a saddle.

Gabe edged forward, the gun in front of him. The darkness was so thick around him he could feel it in his lungs. In the stall the figure ducked down, and Gabe flattened himself against the boards of a stall.

Waiting.

A rattle of metal. Leather straining against itself. The gray shifted feet.

Gabe pushed his breath back and would have sworn he could hear the other fellow breathing. Blinking against the darkness, the old lawman eased away from the wall and back into the aisle.

He never really saw the figure charge him. There was just a shiver of movement, then a sharp, boney shoulder ripping into his chest, hurling the two of them backward, pounding into the dirt and straw.

Gabe's breath clawed out of him in a ripping bark, darkness exploding through him, the wound in his side spraying bone-screaming white pain, tearing his strength from him.

A fist hammered his cheekbone, shoving his face into the dirt. The figure was on top of him, pounding his face with a flurry of fists. Gabe felt himself sinking back into the dirt and the night beyond. Then the figure was gone.

He felt like he'd been on the ground for a long time, and time had blended him into itself, breathing dust through him.

The sound of hooves jerked his head up. He had to think to move. His hand touched metal in the dirt. His pistol. Grasping it, he rolled over. Somebody was pushing the door open. The cool night air washed over Gabe as he got his hands under him, then to his knees. His breath raked through him like burning gravel. He looked up. The horse was moving outside. The figure ahead.

Closing his eyes, Gabe dragged one foot under him, and then the other, straightening himself into a standing position.

Then he ran.

He charged down the dirt floor of the barn, swinging the pistol up. The figure turned, and Gabe caught him in the face with the gun butt, pummeling the figure backward and down.

Gabe grasped for the reins of the gray and tried to steady him.

The figure on the ground sprang up suddenly, his fist stabbing out, catching Gabe just above his wound. The old lawman swung the pistol wide, slamming the figure solidly on the side of the head with a sickening thump, and both of them crashed to the ground. Gabe wrapped his hand with the reins and sat down on his knees. His side felt like somebody had torn him open with a hook. He touched it with his gunhand and smeared his pistol with blood.

A roaring blurred everything, and he didn't know if he passed out or not. It seemed a long time later that he heard Jenny Shannon's voice, and her hands touching him, holding his head up.

"Mr. Early, oh, my God, Mr. Early . . ."

"It's time—I'll—"

Her voice held things together for him and he sat up slightly, reaching out, turning the figure over.

"It's a boy," Jenny said.

Gabe nodded. "McAllister's kid. Stan." Gabe shook his head and spoke to the unconscious youth. "You sure done a job on me, son . . . you surely did. . . . I think you just did Zach's work for him. . . ."

EIGHTEEN

The rain had stopped during the night, drawing itself back into the darkness.

Mitch Prentice rustled from his sleep and peered into a gray, twisting fog. Pine wandered the drifting stillness like soundless century memories. The deputy struggled from his slicker, and standing, he heard the gun first.

He turned as Zach Harper stepped from the fog and trees, the cocked gun leveled at his stomach.

"Damn," Harry Keegan said, materializing through the trees to Mitch's right. "What the hell are you doin' here?"

"My job," the deputy answered. He looked back to Zach. "Figger on shootin' me?" he asked, nodding at the gun.

"I might," the bearded man nodded, and slammed the gun back into leather.

"All right boy," Keegan sniffed, "you can turn around and go home now."

"I'm . . . goin' on," the deputy said. "Ride with you or not, I'm goin' on. It's my job."

"Suppose his bein' a friend don't have nothin' to do with it," Zach said.

"Some," Mitch nodded. "I'm gonna help see he comes back alive. I'm also gonna help see he comes back."

"You're gonna do nothin', pup," Zach sneered. "This was between me and you, Harry. Now send him back."

"It's between me now, too," Mitch broke in. "I'm goin', and you don't have a damn thing to say about it."

Harper's hand dropped to his gun, and Keegan stepped between them.

"Zach," he said, "you can't beat both of us."

Zach stared at him, and nodding, looked past Keegan to the deputy. "One day he won't be standin' there," he said, and turning away, walked back down the hill, the fog drifting around him.

And watching him, Mitch felt something crawl through the quick of his stomach. He could have beaten Zach cold. He could have killed him.

He looked down at his gun. He wasn't playing a game anymore. He might have to kill a man soon.

"Comin'?" asked Keegan.

Mitch jerked a look up.

"What?"

"I said, you comin?"

Mitch looked at his gun again, flexing his hand. "Yeah," he nodded, almost regretfully, "yeah, I'm coming."

After a long time, Gabe was able to walk. Jenny held him, and he made it inside. She put him down on his pallet on the floor and he slipped back into webbed darkness. The heavy scraping of feet on the porch pulled his eyes open again. Jenny was helping the boy inside.

Gabe didn't really think about anything for a while. If it hadn't been for the pain it would have been kind of nice, just laying there, floating, sort of . . .

He felt Jenny opening his shirt again and the wound being cleaned.

"Move," he whispered, forcing his eyes to focus on her. She was frowning deeply, tears hovering in her eyes.

"Have to move," he struggled to say.

"Not for a while," she shook her head.

He rested back. She was right. He knew she was right.

A while. Just a while. Until daylight. Then he had to move. Zach was coming—

The darkness blended over him again. Washing him.

"No," he whispered, fighting the weight in his eyelids. "No," he said aloud, sitting up, then fell back against the wall.

Jenny was beside him again.

"I've got to get out of here," he said in a whispering growl.

Fear darkened her eyes. "Not for a while, Mr. Early."

She stood up and went to the stove. She started a fire and put some coffee on.

Gabe's eyes drifted over the room. The boy was sitting at the table, holding a wet rag against his forehead. Gabe's eyes began to clear, and he could see the boy a little better now. Average-sized, fifteen or sixteen years old, boney; regretful eyes as he touched the wet rag to his forehead again.

"Looks like we done a job on each other," he said to the boy.

Stan's eyes fell. I'm sorry, Mr. Early. I thought you was more of them fellas."

"Sizemore?"

"Don't know any of their names. A lot of them. Wanted fresh horses. Pa said somethin', and one of 'em shot him. Mule-faced fella. The fella that was the leader was awful mad at him."

"When this happen?"

"Day before yesterday."

"How'd you stay alive?"

"I was in the barn. They never saw me. Ran down to the creek after. Don't know how long I was down there. Long time, I guess. I was afraid to come back till last night. Then I seen you."

"You figger we were both outlaws, boy?" he nodded at Jenny.

The boy lowered his eyes shamefully. "There's always Belle Starr."

Gabe smiled, then laughed, laying back. "Yeah, son," he sighed, "there's always Belle Starr." He held his side. "Don't you go feelin' bad, though. You come at me proud."

The boy shrugged, touching his head gingerly.

"What you gonna do now?"

The boy looked up. "How do you mean, Mr. Early?"

"Gonna be a little hard to stay here."

"Yessir," he nodded.

"You got people anywhere?"

"Know some people in Hatchet," the boy said. "Guess I'll head there."

"Long walk," Gabe said.

The boy shrugged. "Twelve miles or so. Done it before." His eyes moved over the room longingly.

Gabe smiled. "Land'll always be here, boy. You can always come back." His smile faded slightly. "Least ways, it'll always seem like it."

"Always wanted to live in town anyhow," the boy said. "Do that for a while. Earn some money and come back."

Gabe's face darkened and he stared at the boy.

"Yeah," he nodded. The scrape of the coffee pot on the stove brought his eyes around to Jenny.

"One more thing, boy," he said.

"Yessir."

"When you get in, send a wagon back for Miss Shannon."

"Yessir," he nodded. "Be glad to."

Gabe smiled up at her. "You be there tonight, ma'am. Now, don't that make you feel some better?"

"Yes," Jenny nodded reluctantly, "yes, that's wonderful."

She worked quickly at the stove, making the coffee, then bacon and gravy and beans. Finding a can of peaches, she opened them, and fed Gabe first. The boy was able to get up and get a plate for himself.

Gabe ate slowly, and she watched him. The fight and the wound opening had weakened him. His movements were jerky and slow. He seemed to have to think about doing them. When he'd finished the food, he looked back up at her. He took coffee from her and smiled with his mouth, but not his eyes.

"How do you feel?" she asked him.

The answer was in his eyes. "I'll be fine, ma'am," he said. "I'll be leavin' at sunup."

She nodded. "What . . . will happen if those men catch up with you?"

Gabe's eyes hardened. "They'll try and take me back," he said.

"But you won't go back, will you?"

His eyes avoided her. "No, ma'am," he answered, "I won't."

She took the plate and stood up and went to the bucket on the worktable. She washed the plate off in the small amount of water in it.

She glanced back at Gabe. He was drinking his coffee. She pulled her eyes away. It was like watching a dead man.

She dried the plate and put it away in the cupboard. Taking the boy's plate, she slammed it down in the water. She rubbed it viciously with the bar of soap, rinsed it, and dried it.

A rustling pulled her eyes around. Gabe was trying to get up. His hands pushed under him, and he lifted himself a little ways, then slumped back down. He would never make it through the door unless someone helped him. It didn't matter if he made it through the door or not. He wouldn't make it much farther anyway.

She rammed the second plate into the cupboard and nearly broke it.

Stan looked up. "Something' wrong, ma'am?"

"No," she snapped. She turned to the stove and made a plate for herself.

Unless someone helped him, she thought again. And shook her head. She was safe now. She could get to Hatchet by tonight and go to work and earn some money and be able to go where she wanted when she wanted . . .

Gabe lay on the pallet for a long time. Then almost heard it. The sunrise. Slow fingers at first. Something errant. An old dreamer rustling leaves. Memories of tomorrow. There was still mostly darkness outside. But Gabe knew it was coming.

He pushed himself up. "Not gonna die here," he murmured, "not here . . ."

Jenny rushed to him. "Wait, Mr. Early. You still have a long time until dawn."

He shook his head. "No," he whispered. "Have to go now."

Pulling his boots on was the hard part. Jenny helped him, then he got his coat on. He checked to see the money was there, then strapped his pistol on and put the cartridge belt over his shoulder. The rifle was still against the wall where he'd put it. Stacker's rifle.

"No, Mr. Early," Jenny pleaded, but helped him up anyway. The boy, Stan, watched them.

"What's wrong, Marshal?" he asked.

"Get me that rifle, boy," Gabe said.

Stan nodded, and brought it to Gabe. Closing his hand around the Sharps, Gabe stood away from Jenny.

The door tilted in front of him. He walked, but his legs didn't seem used to the idea. He had to concentrate on walking. On putting one foot in front of the other until he was outside and on the porch.

It felt good outside. Clean air, darkness, and coming light.

"Stan," he called back to the boy.

"Yessir," the boy answered, coming out of the doorway behind him.

"Got legs like a colt." Gabe cocked his head, "That horse still saddled?"

"Yes," Jenny answered, "I put him back in the barn."

"You bring him to me, boy."

"What's wrong, Mr. Early?"

"Some men after me, son."

The boy nodded, "Yessir," and ran down the steps and across the yard.

"Mr. Early . . ." Jenny's voice was soft.

"Yes, ma'am."

"You won't make it."

Stan came out of the barn, leading the gray.

Gabe smiled back at Jenny. There were tears in her eyes. "Goodbye, Miss Shannon," he said, and turning, he stepped down from the porch.

He'd only taken a few steps when things began to go off to one side again. Like he was walking leaning over. He put the rifle butt down to steady himself, and all of a sudden he was on his knees. Light shimmered around him, whorling, and he fought to stay conscious.

Jenny ran and knelt down beside him. Gabe looked up, shivering.

"Gonna need some help to get on that animal," he said.

She shook her head and looked up at the boy. "There is a wagon in the barn. Will you ready it for me?"

Stan was confused. "What, ma'am?"

She looked at Gabe. You'd better tell him what to do, you know better than I do."

Gabe shook his head in confusion. "What are you doin', anyhow?"

"I'm getting you out of here," she said.

Gabe stared at her, then shook his head. "No, ma'am, I can't let you—"

"I'm not asking you, Mr. Early," she said firmly. "I'm telling you."

Gabe blinked. His eyes stayed on her, then he nodded. "All right, ma'am." He shifted his gaze to the boy. "But a wagon'll never do, not out there in that country."

"I could take you to Coulter, or Hatchet."

"No," he shook his head. "That'd be just as bad. The only chance I've got is out there." He rested his head back, thinking. "No," he said, "a wagon won't do—" He looked at Stan. "You know how to rig a travois, boy?"

"Couple of poles," he nodded, "tarp across it; yessir, I seen it done."

"Then get to it."

"Yessir," the boy nodded and led the gray away.

"You're only buyin' me a little time," he said. "You know that, don't you? They'll catch up to me."

"Maybe not, Mr. Early. Maybe we'll make it."

He smiled, nodding, but not believing it. "Looks like you finally made up your mind to do something, don't it?"

"Looks like it," she nodded.

"How come?"

She brushed a wing of red hair back from her face and smiled. "I've never been to Mexico," she said.

NINETEEN

Harper rode hard. Down the long hills, across the valleys. He rode without stopping. He walked his horse occasionally, then ran him again, always knowing when he was pushing the animal; always knowing when to walk him. He rode out ahead of Keegan and Mitch, as if he weren't really with them.

The sky was clear over them, and they rode down the slopes of new buffalo grass, grama, and bluestem. Mitch watched Harper ride. Tall, straight, seemingly ignoring the black mare under him. It was funny, Mitch thought riding, how much Harper reminded him of Gabe. . . .

After four hours in the saddle, Harper pulled his horse in beside a creek, and dismounting, he loosened the cinch around the horse. "We'll sit for twenty minutes," he said, and holding his black's reins, he sat down under a tree.

Mitch eased down in the shade of a tree near the creek, watching Harper. He was asleep. Or seemed to be.

Keegan sat down next to Harper. He didn't sleep. They stayed that way for twenty minutes.

Then they were in the saddle again.

The mountains streamed south, and Gabe and Jenny followed them toward Mexico. Jenny sat the saddle on the gray, and Gabe rode behind on the travois with a food sack, the ammunition belt, and Stacker's Sharps.

The McAllister house rattled away slowly, the boy Stan watching them. He walked away after a while, then the house was gone behind a ridge line. Gabe rested his head back on the tarp that was carrying him and watched the country pass, knowing that Zach, and the boy, if he was with him, were closing fast. Five or six hours at the most. And that was being cut in half by the minute.

The land sloped and twisted away behind him as they inched through the mesquite.

He eased back on the travois. He felt some better now. Rested. The wound had stopped bleeding, but he was tired. Like twice his forty-eight years.

Forty-eight years old. Twenty of it as a lawman. He was ahead of most. Most never lived through their first year of it. The boy, Mitch, probably would be one of those.

Frowning, he looked forward.

"How you doin', ma'am?"

"Fine," she answered, but the strain quivered her voice.

He nodded and looked back down the falling ground. He wondered if he would ever be coming back. And knew the answer.

His eyes came down to the Sharps riding next to him.

That Sharps, he sighed. It made it seem like old Stacker was running with him.

There was a soft pain when he thought of Stacker. "Fool," Gabe whispered, "damn fool . . ."

"What—"

"Nothin'," he glanced forward self-consciously. And his eyes went back to the Sharps.

"Pick the legs off a snake at two hundred yards," Stacker used to say about that damn buffalo gun.

He could too, Gabe thought, damn thing had a range of up to eighteen hundred yards. . . .

And he smiled suddenly.

"Must be gettin' weak north of the ears," he sighed. "'Course that's the way," he nodded, "I can stop them that way—"

Zach, Keegan, and Mitch rode toward the McAllisters' slowly.

A hundred yards out, Zach stopped his horse, shaking his head.

"Somethin's not right," he said. "Too quiet." He glanced at the deputy. "You notice anything?"

Mitch's eyes combed the buildings and corral.

"No people, no smoke, no horses in the corral."

Zach nodded.

"I'll go straight in," Mitch said.

Zach and Keegan looked at each other.

"Have it your way," Zach shrugged.

They spread. Keegan and Zach hooking, Mitch going in straight. The deputy pulled his rifle from its boot and took it easy. It seemed to take a long time to ride that hundred yards, and on the way in he had more than enough time to wonder about why he'd wanted to do it this way. Out there it seemed like the thing to do. Right now it seemed downright foolish.

He rode by the corral, in between the house and the barn, and reined in his horse. He saw the broken lantern on the porch of the house and eased his horse that way.

Dismounting, he saw the spots of blood near the steps.

It took Gabe a little better than an hour to pick his spot.

They rode on down a long valley, passed a stand of rocks, standing alone, jutting out of the ground like an explosion, then gone again. Well beyond them, Gabe sat up on the travois. There was nothing around the rocks but the wide, flat valley floor. Leaning over one side of the stretcher, he looked ahead and saw the land rising into a sharp ridge.

"Up there," he said to Jenny.

She looked back around.

"What?"

"Up there," he said again, nodding toward the top of the ridge. "That's where we need to head for."

"I don't understand—"

"I'll tell you when we get there—" Gabe cut in. "We ain't got the time right now."

Nodding, Jenny turned the gray up the slope. At the top, he told her to stop, and he sat up on the travois again.

"Yeah," he nodded certainly, and looked back down the slope to the valley. He could see all the way back to the curve of the mountains at the other end of the valley. His eyes dropped to the stand of rocks. They were dead in the open from up here. Around him were a few good-sized boulders. He nodded.

Jenny dismounted clumsily and walked back to him.

"I still don't understand what you're doing, Mr. Early."

"Take the travois on down a bit. Just lead the gray."

"Mr. Early," she began to protest, "I—"

"Just do it, ma'am, then I'll explain."

Frowning, she turned and led the gray down the other side of the slope away from the valley.

He told her to stop when she was below the ridge line.

"*Now* will you tell me what you're doing?" she demanded.

Gabe untied himself from the travois, and sitting up, he held the Sharps.

"Well, ma'am," he said, "I don't imagine you know much about weapons—"

"No," she shook her head.

"This is a Sharps," he said, ".58 caliber. The useful thing about it at this point is that it will carry for something like

eighteen hundred yards. Most rifles are only accurate up to
about three or four hundred. Fella named Billy Dixon
knocked an Indian down at seven-eighths of a mile at a place
called Adobe Walls. That's about fifteen hundred yards—"

"I'm sorry, Mr. Early, I don't see—"

Gabe shifted the rifle in his hand. "No, ma'am, I don't guess
you would." He pointed back toward the top of the ridge.
"Come up here a minute," he said, and they climbed back to
the crest of the ridge. "See those rocks down there?" he pointed
to the stand of rocks.

"Yes—"

"Those rocks are about a mile away, ma'am. There's no
cover around them. When Zach and the boy get to 'em, I'm
gonna open up on 'em. They won't be able to return fire because I'll be out of their range—"

Jenny's face darkened, "You're going to kill them."

"No, ma'am," Gabe shook his head. "I'm gonna slow 'em.
Scatter their animals—"

"You'll kill them."

"Ma'am," Gabe frowned, "that's what I'm tryin' to tell you.
If I scatter their animals, that means I won't have to kill 'em.
If it's Toe-shot—or Zach Harper. This way I can keep
from doin' it. And it's the only hope I've got. This'll give me
the time to get to Crucero Vado. They'll have a helluva time
tryin' to track me through a town."

"I don't like it," she said.

"Neither do I, ma'am. But it's the only thing I can do."

She nodded doubtfully. "I . . . hope it works, then."

Gabe checked the chamber, nodding, "So do I, ma'am."

Zach and Mitch found more blood on a pallet inside the
house.

"He's hit," Zach nodded, and walked back outside.

Keegan rode into the yard and pointed south.

"Trail headin' off that way," he said. "Looks like a horse

pullin' a travois. Lot of tracks around. Man on foot headed toward Hatchet. And there's a woman's tracks."

Zach looked up.

"Woman?"

Keegan nodded.

"McAllister's wife's dead."

Keegan shook his head. "Just tellin' you what I saw." He looked around. "Wonder where McAllister is."

Zach shrugged. "Don't matter," he said. "Looks like you hit Gabe back in town. Blood in there. The travois is likely for him." Walking to his horse, he mounted up. Mitch did the same.

"Remember," Keegan said, "he gets his chance to come in."

Zach turned his horse out, kicking him south.

TWENTY

Gabe and Jenny walked back down to the travois. Jenny took the food sack from the stretcher, and spreading a cloth on the ground, she went to work making sandwiches from the meat and bread the McAllister boy had given her.

Gabe fished a three-foot leather thong from the saddlebags, and taking it, the Sharps, and the cartridge belt, he climbed back to the crest of the ridge. Finding a clump of rock, he sat down, laid the cartridge belt to one side, then tied one end of the leather thong to the barrel and the other around the stock. That done, he looped the thong around his upper left arm, and placing the stock in his shoulder, he stretched the leather out taut. He brought the rifle down and took up a little slack in the leather. The hand holding the barrel usually weaves some, throwing the aim off. By tightening the leather across his arm and keeping it taut, he braced the arm, and cut part of the blood off at the same time, making his arm heavy, providing a base to fire from.

He unwrapped his arm and checked the Sharps. Stacker had kept it spotless. Gabe put the rifle down and moved his eyes back to the valley floor, then farther back to the line of mountains, the way they'd come. That would be the way Zach and Toe-shot would come too. Around those hills and right down the valley floor.

Jenny brought the sandwiches up, and they ate. Clouds washed down the sky. Across the ragged mountains, and the peak blended with them. Blue. Black, then brown again as they passed. A lark called, and the sun felt good on Gabe.

"How do you feel, Mr. Early?"

"Good, ma'am. Rest is doin' me the best of all. And that good food," he nodded.

He smiled at her, and then moved his eyes back down to the line of hills. Fixing them on the place Zach would make the turn.

Gabe pulled his tobacco from his coat pocket and frowned. That was all of it. He slipped the Winesap into his mouth and chewed slowly.

"How far is it yet, Mr. Early?"

"Mexico? Not ten, fifteen miles. Crucero Vado is on down a bit. Should be there tomorrow morning. Should have been there tonight," he frowned, then smiled it away. "But tomorrow'll do."

"What will you do then?"

"Rest there a day, I guess, take out the next mornin'. Bright'n early. Zach and the boy won't take forever catchin' up their horses."

"You're certain they're following you, aren't you, Mr. Early?"

Gabe nodded. "Yes, ma'am," he said, "I know it."

"Maybe the boy isn't. Maybe he decided not to come after you."

"No, ma'am," Gabe shook his head, "more I think about it, more certain I am about it. The boy has a certain way of doin' things. He's after me, all right. Could be he's not with Zach. But I'd bet he is. Anyhow, I know he's after me."

Jenny shook her head. "It's insane," she whispered.

"Ma'am?"

"Doesn't friendship mean anything? Or love?"

Gabe nodded slowly, "'Course it does, ma'am. But there's always more to it than that."

Shadows moved down the valley floor. Gabe's fingers sweated against the wood of the stock. The sun pressed into his face and back and side. Quail drifted lace against the sky.

Down the slope, the gray shifted his feet and chewed on bluestem. Jenny lay near Gabe's feet asleep, her red-blond hair awash on the ground. He touched it gently, then looked back at the turn of the hills.

It was funny. In the spring a man could only remember spring. He remembered . . .

The first figure rounded the term.

Gabe put the Sharps down, and making a peephole of his hand, he made sure.

One. Two. No, three of them. Three of them coming fast, black against the brown of the valley floor, like a memory of movement. Riding.

Gabe bellied down on the grass and dirt and watched them come. He spread the cartridge belt out next to him.

It took them less than half an hour to cross the valley. Then they seemed to come awfully fast at the end.

Squinting, Gabe nodded and frowned.

He could see Mitch's blond hair fingering down from under his hat.

"Goddammit, Toe-shot," he murmured, "when'll you ever get some sense?"

And there was Zach, riding his black hard. And Harry Keegan.

They hammered toward the rocks bearing down on them. Gabe glanced back at the sleeping woman. He touched her gently on the shoulder.

"Ma'am," he said.

Jenny rustled and her eyes came awake. Sleepy and soft.

"Better move down, ma'am."

Her eyes jerked up the slope.

"They're coming?" she said.

He nodded. "Yes, ma'am. Now do like I said, there might be some lead up here. Accidental."

Jenny started to say something, but frowning in its place, she turned and walked back down the slope to the gray.

Gabe's eyes stayed with her a long moment, then turned back to the valley floor.

Looping the leather thong around the upper half of his left arm, he wedged the rifle stock down into his shoulder and sighted on the riding men.

Fifteen yards to the rocks.

Gabe pulled the rifle down, levering the trigger guard, breaking the chamber open. He slipped a shell into the chamber, and pulling the trigger guard closed, he placed the stock back into his shoulder.

Zach was in the lead. Riding easy. Mitch was right behind. Then Harry.

They came up on the stand of rocks and passed it.

Gabe pulled the hammer of the Sharps back gently, and sighting down the barrel, he squeezed the trigger.

The crash of the shot shattered the air, rocking Gabe. He lifted himself up to see a plume of dust blossom to the left of Mitch. Quickly Gabe levered out the empty brass, reloaded, and put another shot just in front of Zach.

The black reared, screaming, kicking backward. Like a practiced piece of machinery, Gabe loaded and fired the Sharps again, sending another shot under the black. Then one off the rocks.

Beneath Mitch his horse reeled wildly. Fighting to stay in the saddle, he buried his hand in the horse's mane. Another shot blew away a hunk of rock. Mitch's horse sidestepped, twisting, swinging Mitch over to one side. Pitching out of the saddle, Mitch slammed into the ground with his shoulder, then was jerked out flat by the pull of the reins. He let go of the leather and let his horse run.

Above him, a blur of black, mixed with the sound of screaming.

Another shot ripped off the boulders.

Mitch raised himself on one knee and stumbled, then got up again, and running, fell again. Shaking his head, he had a mouthful of dirt. He got to his feet again, staggering into the cover of the rocks, then slumped down, spitting dirt and grass out of his mouth, and looked back out in the open.

Zach was still aboard the black, but the animal was all over the place. All hell and hooves and spit.

Harry was on the ground, pulling his dun toward him, trying to keep him from running.

Lead splashed into the rock. Zach's black reeled, standing up on her hind legs, twisting around in midair. Zach pumped his feet out of the stirrups, pummeling to the ground like a man on a slide. He hit hard on his chest, and pushed up on his hands and knees, cawing for air through the dust. One of the black's hooves caught him in the hip, tumbling him through the dust. Zach's head came up like it was coming through water. He got up again and ran stumbling toward the rocks.

A slug ripped off the boulders next to Mitch, blowing splinters off in a wad, and Zach dived in beside the young deputy. He lay there a moment, then sitting up, he looked at Mitch.

"The bastard," he choked. "That's Ald's Sharps."

Two more quick shots drove them farther down into the rocks.

Swearing, and tearing his eyes up, Mitch realized for the first time that Keegan wasn't with them.

"Harry?" Mitch called, and looked back into the flurry of dust and horses.

Keegan pulled himself out of the dirt shaking his head. Above and around him, the horses were screaming, and the dust was so thick it blinded him.

Another slug hit the rocks.

He blinked his eyes.

Gabe was shooting at him. His friend.

Crawling to his knees and shaking his head violently, he drew his pistol.

"Sonofabitch," he growled. Gabe was his friend. And he was shooting at him.

Thumbing the hammer of the Colt, Keegan fired up the ridge. Next to him a form bolted, kicking. He fired again.

"Gabe—" he screamed, firing again. And again, the sound of it mixing with the rising screams of the horses. Still firing, he ran toward the ridge.

Suddenly Zach's black mare materialized out of the dust, looming up before the lawman on his hind legs.

Then falling. His long, night-colored legs driving down, exploding into him.

And the hooves crushed his skull.

In the rocks, Mitch watched.

"Harry," he whispered, starting to stand up, but Zach pulled him back down.

Through the dust Mitch could see the U.S. marshal doubled like a child sleeping, except his arm was twisted behind him and the side of his head was gone.

On the ridge, Gabe had seen Harry thrown, then heard the firing.

"Harry?" he said, and the Sharps dropped slightly. "Get out of there, you damn fool, those horses are spooked enough—"

There was a lot of dust, and then horses running, and a wad of color crumbled by the outcropping.

"Harry?" Gabe squinted down the slope. It couldn't be, he thought. It couldn't . . .

The dust lingered, then thinned like water clearing, and he could see clearer. The wad of color down there was a man.

"Jesus, Harry," he trembled, "what the hell did you do that for?"

A shudder hammered through Gabe, and a dizziness flushed him, blurring his vision. Shaking his head, he looked at the dead man.

Without thinking, he levered the brass, reloaded, and fired again. Then, as if he realized for the first time he was holding a rifle, he looked down at it.

"My God," he murmured, "my God."

He wiped the sweat from his face, blinking. Then raising the rifle again, he reloaded and fired.

He seemed to sit there a long time. With memory, the smell of power, and the dust.

Then he pushed away from the rise suddenly, lying down low on his belly and backing away. He stood up below the crest, and his legs were weak. He walked wobbly-legged back down the slope to Jenny.

He lay down on the travois wordlessly.

"Mr. Early . . . !"

"Let's go," he said.

TWENTY-ONE

Mitch and Zach sat hunched deep in the rocks. Zach peered up at the sky, wiping sweat from his face.

"Nearly five," he said.

Mitch nodded, and Zach glanced back up over the rocks toward the ridge.

"How long's it been now since he fired last?"

"Hour. Hour and a half," Mitch answered.

The big rancher drifted his eyes over their small place in the rocks. The air was foul with dust and sweat. He took off his hat and ran his fingers through his hair.

He shook his head, "Can't sit in this goddamn stand for the rest of our lives," he sighed, and stood up.

"And if he's still up there?" Mitch asked from the ground.

"Then I'll get my ass blown off. I'm not sitting here any longer." He looked down at the deputy. "How 'bout it, son?"

Mitch looked up at Zach, then out at the ridge. He shook his head wearily.

"Not too fond of this place either," he said, standing up. His insides were shaking so bad, for a second he thought he would wet his pants. He smiled at Zach. He wouldn't let him know he was scared.

Mitch shot a glance up the ridge, then stepped out into the open ahead of Zach and hesitated.

He cleared his throat as Zach followed.

Both men stared at Keegan's crumpled form for a moment. Mitch walked over to him and straightened his legs, then put his arms to his side. He took off his coat and put it over the dead man's face.

"Let's go," Zach said.

Nodding, Mitch turned. "You figure those horses have headed for McAllisters'?"

"No other water that I know of."

Mitch looked back. "Why the hell did he do that?"

"Don't matter," Zach said. "Gabe killed him."

"Harry could have done the sensible thing."

Zach faced the deputy.

"What the hell does he have to do—massacre a whole god-damn town for you to see what he is?"

Mitch frowned, and started to say something, then shook his head.

"Don't matter," the deputy sighed, "Gabe's won. Once he goes through Crucero Vado and across the Rio Caballo, there ain't no way you'll track him."

"I'll find one," Zach said, and started walking, striding out back down the valley.

Gabe and Jenny stopped after sundown. The old lawman had been quiet since the shooting back at the ridge. Jenny tried to talk to him several times, but his responses had been short, usually one word.

They came into a small stand of yuccas, and stepping down from the gray, Jenny started back to help Gabe from the travois.

"I can do it," he nodded, standing up by himself and, taking blankets from the travois, he sat down against a rock.

Jenny watched him, then gathered wood and started a fire. With that done, she made sandwiches from the food they had left, and, turning to Gabe, held one out to him.

Gabe shook his head.

"Not right now, thank you, ma'am."

Nodding, she put the food into the lap of her skirt.

"What about those men?" she asked.

"They . . . they'll be a while catchin' up their animals," he said. "If they decide to come on to Crucero Vado, they'll be at least a day and a half doin' it."

"Then it worked?"

His eyes came around to hers. "Yes, ma'am," he replied quietly, "it worked." His eyes moved back to the darkness.

Jenny watched him, but he didn't seem to know it, or even realize she was there. She started to eat a sandwich, then put it down again.

"What is it, Mr. Early?"

Touching her eyes, he smiled humorlessly. "Beginnin' to believe women do have another sense," he shook his head. "Harry . . . Keegan got himself killed back there—"

She almost dropped the plate.

"Did you—"

"No," he frowned, "no, I didn't kill him. Not directly. Horse trampled him." He was silent for a moment. "I didn't shoot him, but I killed him in a way." His face stiffened. "Goddammit, why didn't he run for cover . . . damn fool . . . why the hell? . . ."

The fire snapped in front of them, rippling the flames.

"Why anything, Mr. Early?"

Gabe looked up. "What, ma'am?"

Jenny shrugged. "Sometimes there are no reasons for things. Sometimes there are no reasons for people."

Gabe smiled softly. "There are reasons, Miss Shannon. People make them. And if you're talkin' about yourself, you don't know it yet, but you're nearly ready for Lucky Callahan. All it will take is makin' up your mind to it."

Puzzlement narrowed her eyes. "Who is . . . ?"

Gabe laughed. "Story I told Mitch not long ago. About a fella I knew a long time ago. Mean . . ." he hesitated, trying to think of a polite word, "sort of fella. Could whip ever'body in six states and two provinces of Canada. All the cowhands'd get drunk and want to fight him. Whipped 'em all. Till one day a fella went up against him sober. Beat Lucky fair. It was

all in knowing what you wanted and how to go about it." He
nodded. "You'll do all right, ma'am."

"And the boy?"

"Mitch," Gabe shrugged. "Someday he'll have to make up
his mind too."

She nodded, "Yes, I guess, he will." She looked at the food
in her lap. "You should eat something."

"No," he said, "not now."

A wind brushed across them, and Jenny shivered.

"Another blanket here, ma'am."

She took it, wrapping it around herself. "I don't want to
sleep yet," she said. "But I think I will rest a minute. . . ."

A long time later she stirred in her sleep, spilling the food
out on the ground. She said something Gabe couldn't understand, and reaching out, he pulled her to him, and sitting up,
he held her. The night wandered above them, the stars map-
ping questions no one would ever think to ask.

Gabe held her, feeling her breathe, quieter now. He
thought about killing, and he thought about Jenny Shannon's
breathing, and her warmth. She stirred, and he held her
tighter. She hovered next to him, and he held her until morning came.

TWENTY-TWO

Mitch opened his eyes thinking he'd heard something. Blinking, he sat forward, away from the rock he'd used as a back-
rest during the night. A light haze drifted the hill, scattering
the dark morning light. Next to him Zach Harper was still
sleeping.

Mitch reached out to Zach to wake him, and the sound rasped again. A scrape of metal. Hesitating, Mitch stood up and peered down the slope. Then he saw the flicker of movement. Down at the base of the hill. It was a horse. Grazing on a patch of grass. A dun. Keegan's horse.

Shivering in the morning cold, the deputy pushed himself to his feet quietly and eased down the slope toward the animal. The horse's head pumped up. Mitch stopped, trying to keep from even breathing. The horse dipped his head back down, and Mitch slipped his hat off his head, starting toward the animal again. The horse's head eased up, and Mitch kept walking, jiggling the hat slightly.

"Come on, now, fella," he said gently, "come on, you pea-brained, hard-backed, rock-headed fool." He lulled his voice, "Oats. Hope you've had plenty of oats from a hat, fella, I just hope . . ." he kept talking, holding the hat out to the horse.

The dun backed, and Mitch forced a smile into his voice, jiggling the hat a little more.

The dun watched him come. Mitch moved softly on the shale. A few feet from the horse, he stretched out, reaching for the dangling reins, holding the hat out at the same time.

The horse jammed his nose into the hat and Mitch grabbed the leather. The dun turned to run, pumping his back feet. Mitch dropped the hat, charging him, diving for the saddle horn, fastening desperate hands on it. The dun reeled around, swinging Mitch with him, slamming the deputy's back with his neck. Mitch barked a cough, then dragged himself back and up into the saddle.

The dun stood still snorting, shaking his head harshly. Probably figured that was enough exercise for one morning, Mitch nodded. If he did, Mitch agreed. Leaning in the saddle, he scraped sweat and dirt from his face with his hand.

"Helluva thing to do before breakfast," he decided aloud, and keeping an eye on the dun, he dismounted, and got hold of the other rein.

He turned back up the hill. Zach stood above him, watching,

his eyes on the horse. Mitch didn't like the look in his eyes. They were too concentrated, too careful.

"Keegan's horse," Mitch said.

Zach nodded without saying anything.

"I'll see to catchin' up the other horses," Mitch said, and felt the tremor in his voice. Zach's eyes stayed on him as he turned to mount the animal.

"Just a second, son," Zach said.

Mitch looked back.

"If I take that mount," Zach nodded at the dun," I can make Crucero Vado tonight. He can save me half a day right now."

Mitch shook his head.

"I said I was gonna be there when you caught up with him, and I am—"

Zach nodded slowly. "Looks like we've come down to it, don't it, son." He walked down the hill toward Mitch.

"Looks like," Mitch nodded.

Zach stopped six feet away from him. The hammer thong on his pistol was loose. Zach shook his head. "You gonna die for a horse, son. It don't seem worth it, does it?"

"It's up to you."

Zach smiled, his hand jerking back to the pistol—then stopped just as suddenly.

The deputy's pistol was already out, cocked and leveled at his belly.

Zach's eyes pulled from the gun to Mitch's face. It was hard, lined like rock.

The deputy stepped toward Zach, the gun held out in front of him, the knuckles white around the grip. Zach held his hand as still as possible as Mitch stared at him. The pistol lowered a little, then more, drifting back to its leather.

Mitch turned and mounted the dun.

"You . . . didn't learn much from Gabe."

Mitch shrugged. "Maybe it's just beginning to sink in." He turned the horse. "I'll catch up your animal—"

"You comin' back?" Zach asked incredulously.

Mitch nodded without saying anything.

"You gonna still try and take him back?"

Mitch shook his head. "No . . . not that anymore. You'll catch up with him someday. I can't kill you—so I'll just have to be there when you do." He spurred the dun. "Head for McAllister's," he called back. "I'll meet you on the way."

TWENTY-THREE

Gabe finished the last of his coffee, and standing, checked his side.

"Think we can do away with the travois," he said to Jenny.

She smiled, looking up from the side of the fire. "You well enough to ride?"

"Be best that way," he nodded. "If Sizemore's men are in Crucero Vado I don't want them noticing me anymore'n usual." He smiled gently at the woman, "Pretty soon now you'll be in some more peaceful surroundings. Get you back to Hatchet."

"How far is it to Crucero Vado now?"

"This afternoon sometime," Gabe nodded. "Not far. Not far at all."

They rode double, down the edge of the mountains through dry, rough country.

It was late in the afternoon when he saw the town. First ripples on the horizon, then shapes out at the end of a long flat. Beyond the town were the mountains.

"That's it," Gabe said. "Crucero Vado."

"You mean we're in Mexico?"

Gabe smiled. "Have been for about the last twenty miles. Least ways, that's how far it's supposed to be to the border. Nothin' to mark it."

Jenny smiled too. "Mexico," she nodded, smiling. "I've never been to a foreign country."

Gabe pointed to the mountains. "That's where I'm bound, Miss Shannon," he said. "Little place in there. Gonna find me some pasture." He looked around at her, a grin tugging his lips. It was one of the few times she'd ever seen him smile. "I hate to say it," he winked, "but I think we made it."

It took them another hour to cover the distance to the pueblo.

Adobe shacks rose up around them, giving off a musty smell mixing with the odor of heat, dust, people, open market, and rotting meat.

They were halfway down the street when Gabe saw the rider come from between two shacks, turn his horse, and ride into the center of town.

"Woody knows we're here," Gabe said.

They rode down the street and into the plaza that was the center of town.

He jerked his horse to a stop.

A well stood in the center of the plaza. On it hung the bloodied uniform of a gendarme, a Mexican policeman.

"What is it?" Jenny asked.

"Nothing," Gabe said.

"Is something wrong?" Jenny asked.

Gabe blinked, looking back around. "No—" he answered, and nudged the horse.

The hotel was the only wooden building in the plaza; two stories, and it looked like it leaned a little. Half of it was a cantina, with tables scattered in front beneath the shade of an awning. The blacksmith shop was on one side; on the other was a street leading to the Rio Caballo and the mountains.

Gabe counted seven horses in front of the hotel.

From the cantina it sounded like a fiesta was in progress. Outside, beneath the awning, one man sat quietly.

Gabe reined up in front of the hotel, and dismounting, he looked at the man sitting off by himself, a bowler hat pushed back on his head, wearing a coat even in the coming heat. There was a bulge beneath the coat.

I know him, Gabe thought, I—

And remembering, he pulled his eyes away.

Gabe helped Jenny down and tried not to look like he was moving too fast as they went inside. The noise grew louder, and the clerk behind the desk looked up at them nervously as they came through the door. His bald head glistened with a paste of sweat.

"*Sí*, señor," he attempted a smile.

"A room for me and the lady."

"*Uno cuarto, sí.*"

Gabe shook his head. "One for me, and one for the lady."

A nervous tremor jerked through the clerk's lips. "Sorry, señor."

A bottle crashed beyond the swinging doors and a roar of laughter followed. Gabe eyed the door, and the clerk handed him the keys quickly. "I would stay away from the bar if I were you, señor," he said quietly. "It is not safe to go in there now."

"Trouble?"

The clerk nodded. "They have thrown out the bartender. When the gendarme comes they beat him very bad. He wakes up and they beat him again. They say they do not like the *policia*. They make him crawl through the plaza to the river. Hang his uniform outside. He is lucky they don't kill him."

"Lucky he didn't let his pride talk for him." Gabe frowned, shifting the Sharps and taking the keys from the clerk.

"We'll need baths, and the lady'll need some fresh clothes. Can you see to that?"

The clerk nodded. "The bath for the lady is upstairs. For you is in the back."

"The livery?"

"In the back also."

Gabe nodded, and taking Jenny's arm, they went upstairs. They walked down the hall. At the far end was another doorway. Gabe checked the keys and picked the one farthest from the stairs. He opened the door for Jenny and followed her in.

Without hesitation, he crossed the room and looked down at the uniform, then at the awning. He couldn't see Sizemore.

"That noise downstairs," Jenny said, "that was the man you told me about. Sizemore."

Gabe looked around. "As a matter of fact, that was him sittin' down there in front."

"The man at the table?"

Gabe nodded.

"Do you know him?"

Gabe rubbed his nose. "No," he answered slowly. "But I've met him. Porch of the Holman House the night of the robbery."

"Then he'll know you."

Gabe shook his head. "Don't think so. It was dark. Only reason I know him is by that bowler hat and the shoulder gun. Shoulda known that night—"

Jenny's face darkened. "Will there be trouble?"

Gabe considered it. "No, ma'am, I don't think so. Just take things easy . . ." He looked at the woman. "Right now," he sighed, "I'm gonna take to gettin' a bath."

"Yes," Jenny closed her eyes thankfully, "I've never been this long without one."

Gabe left the Sharps in his room and checked the back door. It led downstairs to the livery. Frowning, he walked outside and down the stairs. It was one way of not seeing Woody.

There was an alley behind the hotel, and one between the hotel and the blacksmith shop. A boy sat on the ground in front of the livery. His dark eyes came up to Gabe. He was close to twelve, Gabe judged, dressed in white hand-made shirt and pants. No shoes.

Gabe ambled across the alley to him.

"This for the hotel?" he asked the boy in Spanish.

The boy stood up. "*Sí*, señor."

Gabe took out a dollar. "My horse is the gray around front. Get him for me, will you?"

"*Sí*, señor," the boy nodded and started off.

"That the bathhouse?" Gabe pointed to the building next to the livery.

"No, señor, the *bañadero* is there," he pointed to the next building. "I will get your horse now."

Gabe watched the boy go around the building, then turned toward the bathhouse.

A ripple of laughter drifted from the *casa de putas*, and a form appeared in the doorway. A big man with a face like a mule. He sagged against the frame, still laughing, then stopped when he saw Gabe. Gabe kept walking, and the mule-faced man's eyes followed him until he went into the bathhouse. Gabe closed the door behind him. In the *casa de putas*, he could hear a woman's voice, then a slap.

Gabe frowned. That one would be Candy. Wanted for everything from shakedowns to murder. The man Stan had said had killed his father. Nice folks, Gabe thought, and shaking his head, he undressed and took his bath. Afterward, he trimmed his mustache and took a good look at his wound. It was better. He smiled. Tomorrow morning he would be headed for those mountains.

Dressing again, Gabe went back outside, reaching for his pocket knife and tobacco. He found the silver-handled knife, then remembered he had no more tobacco. He walked down the alley and around to the front of the hotel. He took the towel and soap back inside and put them on the clerk's desk.

He nodded toward the door to the bar. "Any tobacco in there?" he asked the clerk.

The clerk's eyes jerked up.

"I think so, señor, but I wouldn't—"

Gabe stared at the doors. No rowdy had ever kept him out of a place yet. Not till now, he frowned. That was yesterday. Things were different now.

The sounds from the bar seemed to follow him up the stairs.

TWENTY-FOUR

Sitting by the window in his room, Gabe stared down at the uniform on the well and listened to the noise drifting up from the cantina. The first filter of dusk began to brush the air before he realized what time it was. Picking up his hat, he walked next door and tapped gently.

Jenny opened the door and smiled at seeing Gabe. She wore a new print dress, and her hair fell to her shoulders, gleaming like there were fires in it. She smelled of soap and clean cloth.

Gabe had to think to speak. "Mighty . . . fine," he nodded his approval.

She tipped her head shyly. "Thank you, sir."

Gabe took her arm and they went downstairs to the lobby. They were halfway across when Woody Sizemore pushed through the swinging doors from the cantina. Gabe stiffened, his hand tightening on Jenny's arm as he edged by the outlaw. Woody half glanced at him, then again as Gabe and Jenny walked on by, and out the door.

"Did he know you?" Jenny asked when they were in the plaza.

"No," Gabe said, "most likely not."

They crossed to a small restaurant and went inside. Gabe picked a table out of line with the windows, and a boy waited on them. Keeping his eyes on the door, Gabe ordered for them both and instructed the boy to go light on the *salsa* for the lady.

As the boy walked away, Gabe looked at Jenny. Her hand touched the cameo around her neck self-consciously, and Gabe nodded at it.

"That cameo, ma'am," Gabe said.

Jenny glanced down, dropping her fingers from it.

"Habit," she said.

"Where'd you get it?"

"My father gave it to me. Why?"

Gabe shook his head. "Nothin'. You seem to value it a lot. Figure anything your Pa would give you, you'd want to be rid of."

Jenny glanced down at it again and shrugged. "Yes, I suppose." She picked a dry tortilla out of the basket on the table. "Are these like bread?" she asked, and Gabe knew she didn't want to talk about the cameo anymore.

He smiled, shrugging, "A bit. Go ahead and bite in."

She placed the tortilla carefully in her mouth and bit down gently. The tortilla split apart and she had to catch part of it to keep it off the table, then chewing the noisy cornmeal, she tried to look as ladylike as possible. Gabe started laughing and tried to keep from it, putting his hand over his mouth. Jenny saw him and started laughing too, with a mouthful of tortilla. She continued to laugh and chew at the same time.

Wiping tears from his eyes, Gabe saw Woody Sizemore come through the door. The smile slipped away from Gabe's mouth, and he looked to Jenny.

Gabe knew Woody saw him and was watching him as he ambled to a table and sat down. Gabe didn't look at him, but knew the outlaw's eyes were on him.

The boy took Woody's order, then returning from the back, he brought Gabe and Jenny's food. Tacos, enchiladas,

rice, *salsa*, and tortillas. He placed it down on the table, and
Woody stood up and crossed the floor to their table.

Gabe nodded to him. "Help you?"

Woody smiled, and nodded, "You know, I was sitting
there havin' a drink this afternoon and saw you then again
just now. . . ." He shook his head, "Well, to make a long
story short, be damned if I don't know you from someplace.
The both of you." He grinned, "And in my line of work, I
have to stay up with things like that."

"What line of work you in?"

"Ahh . . . well, to put it polite, I ain't exactly honest. Law-
wise, that is."

Gabe nodded. "Could be that's how we know each other.
I have some to do with the law."

"Just the feelin' I've seen you lately."

Gabe shrugged. "Been here and there."

Sizemore rubbed his nose, "Well, maybe it'll come back to
me. Join me for a drink later if you like—'cross the street
there."

"I'll do that," Gabe nodded.

As Sizemore walked out the door, Gabe sighed a long
breath and shook his head.

"Hope I don't have to do that too often."

Jenny made no effort to hide her concern. "What are you
going to do?"

"Have a drink," Gabe shrugged. "It's no time to be rude
to anybody. Especially Woody Sizemore. He's still trying to
remember where he saw me. Wants me where he can keep an
eye on me. Don't go. He'll know somethin's wrong."

"How do you know he won't kill you?"

Gabe shook his head. "I don't. I don't think he will, though,
unless he remembers me."

They finished their meal, and Gabe walked Jenny back to
her room. At the door he hesitated, then putting his hand in
his coat, he brought out the envelope. He fingered into it and
pulled out several bills.

"Here," he said handing them to her, "is a hundred or so dollars. It'll get you to . . . Hatchet or wherever you want to go."

Jenny shook her head, "No, Mr. Early, I can't. I'd be obligated to you, and I—"

"I'm obligated to you, Miss Shannon," he cut her off.

She nodded slowly, taking the money, looking up at him. "All right," she said, "if you'll take something in return." And reaching up, she took the cameo from around her neck and handed it to him.

"No, ma'am," he protested, "I—"

"I don't need it anymore, Mr. Early."

A smile creased his eyes. "No, ma'am," he said, taking it from her, "I don't reckon you do." He glanced down at it, then slipped it into his vest pocket. "Thank you." He started to turn, then said, "I . . . I'll most likely be gone before you're up in the mornin'. . . I . . ." he cleared his throat. It wasn't coming out right. "Hell," he muttered, "you're a helluva woman, Miss Shannon."

Jenny managed to smile. "You're a helluva man, Mr. Early."

He touched her hand quickly and nodded. "Goodbye," he said, and turned away. He heard her voice soft behind him and then the brush of the door closing.

Gabe pushed his way through the double doors into the cantina, and Woody waved him to the bar.

Gabe threaded into the half-lit room, which smelled of smoke, sweat, whiskey, urine, and memory. There were mostly gringos. A couple of Mexicans. All wore guns. Four women roamed around among the men, but Gabe could feel the eyes of the men following him to the bar.

He recognized some of them. Poster faces. German Bob. Light-skinned, pale. Liked to use a shotgun. A soft-faced boy named Reno. Wore two guns. Had killed ten men at last count. Right now he was giving a whore a bad time. At the

table next to him was Jesus Morales. Liked knives and had
never quite lived up to his name. The mule-faced one, Candy,
stood at the bar watching Gabe closely. The rest Gabe didn't
know. Probably just as well.

Gabe bellied up to the bar next to Sizemore.

"Earl," Gabe said, holding out his hand, "Earl Prentice."
He took the first name that came to mind.

"Prentice," Sizemore nodded, taking the offered hand hesitantly. "Woody Sizemore."

Gabe blinked and looked around. "Sizemore," he nodded,
"that explains it. You're a famous man."

"Got no qualms about drinkin' with the lower side of soci-
ety?"

Gabe shrugged. "That's what I thought we all were down
here."

Sizemore chuckled. "Could be," he nodded, eying Gabe.
"Still think I know you from someplace. Your woman looks
familiar too."

Gabe smiled. "She looks familiar to a lot of people."

"I can see why," Sizemore mused. "No offense."

"None taken," Gabe said. "Any tobacco back there?"

"Think so—" he turned to the mule-faced man. "Candy,"
he said, "see to some tobacco."

"Ain't no goddamn barkeep," Candy grumbled grudgingly,
but went behind the bar anyway, found the tobacco, and
handed it to Gabe.

Woody poured two drinks. "Well," the outlaw grinned,
"have at it. This stuff'll raise blood blisters on a boot."

Gabe downed his drink.

"Give you a snake with ever' glass," he shivered.

"Smashed and poured in," Woody swallowed with difficulty. "Makes me feel like a centipede walked across me."

"Has to, to make you drink it."

Woody agreed with a nod and eyed Gabe again. "Look like
a gambler," he observed. "Don't do much with your hands."

"Not much," Gabe leaned on the bar.

"What line you in?"

Gabe thought for a moment, then smiled with a slow shrug, "I could always lie to you, Woody. But if I was a lawdog, or a bounty man, I would have come with more help than a red-haired woman."

A little shocked at Gabe's directness, Woody found himself smiling sheepishly, "Guess you would have, at that."

"'Sides," Gabe glanced around the room, "the odds don't look so good." He poured himself another drink. "No," he shook his head, "to be right truthful with you, I'm headed back into the mountains. Gonna watch the grass grow and get fat."

Woody's face softened slightly. "That right? Thought about it a couple of times myself. Ever goddamn waddie between here and the south end of hell thinks about it, I guess." He pushed his bowler hat back and scratched his hair. "Even tried it once," he laughed rememberingly. "Got bored. Ain't that the damnedest thing? I got bored." He sipped his whiskey. "Ain't a lot to be said for a cat-eyed life—but it ain't borin'."

"Man gets used to things," Gabe said, nearly more to himself than to Woody. "Hard to unlearn certain things."

Woody's mouth pushed a frown through his face. "Ahh," he groaned, "to tell you the truth, it's even gettin' borin' around here. Hurrahed the only law out. Not a helluva lot to do but catch crabs. That's always kind of interestin'—"

"Well," Gabe nodded, "guess I'll be hittin' it. Long way to ride tomorrow."

"Yeah," Woody sipped the last of his whiskey, "good luck with your grass growin'. Hope you make do."

"Thanks," Gabe turned away, "I will."

Walking toward the door, Gabe smiled. Another eight hours and he would have it made.

It was well after dark when Mitch drew in his animal.

"Good a place as any," he called to Zach.

The bearded man turned in the darkness. "Ain't stoppin'," he said.

Mitch frowning, sighing. "Jesus, Zach, you can't ride this country at night. End up killin' you and a perfectly good horse at the same time."

Wordlessly Zach strapped his black out, hooves rattling against the sharp rocks.

"Damn," the deputy grumbled, and followed him. "You figger on bein' there by mornin', I take it?"

"You still comin'?"

"He's gonna have his chance," the deputy said.

"He'll get it," Zach nodded, strapping his horse harder. "He'll get it real soon now."

TWENTY-FIVE

Dawn was graying the windows when Gabe got out of bed. Walking to the window, he could see the mountains.

He smiled, and turning, his eyes fell on the bloodied uniform hanging on the crossbeam of the well. His stomach twisted, and he shook his head. It wasn't any of his business anymore.

He dressed quickly, and after gathering what he had, he walked into the hall. Hesitating for a moment, he looked back at Jenny's door, then walked on to the back stairs. The smell of breakfast mingled with the rustle of people and animals as he walked down the steps and into the small livery.

Coming into the barn he saw the livery boy, Miguel, asleep on a mound of hay. The old lawman shook his head softly.

"Miguelito," he whispered, and crossing the dirt floor, he leaned down and placed a ten-dollar gold piece in the boy's shirt pocket. Then he turned to his horse, saddled him quietly, and led him out of the livery, down the alley around the hotel, and across the plaza to the *restaurante*.

Gabe tied the gray at the rack, went inside, and sat down in front of the window.

A woman came and he ordered coffee and eggs. She brought the coffee and the eggs with a mound of chili and a stack of tortillas.

Smiling, Gabe nodded and picked up his fork.

The rattle of a running horse in the plaza tugged his eyes away from the eggs and to the window.

One of the men Gabe had seen in the saloon last night with Sizemore rode in from the north. He dismounted while the horse was still moving and ran into the hotel.

Resting the fork back on the table, Gabe picked up his coffee and watched the hotel. An old feeling crawled into the quick of his stomach and along the back of his neck at the same time.

Two minutes later the rider came back out of the hotel followed by Reno, Candy, Jesus, and Woody. Woody and Reno were just finishing strapping on their guns, and Woody was saying something. Gabe pushed himself away from the table and walked to the door of the *restaurante*.

Woody finished talking, and the rider nodded. Gabe could only hear part of what he was saying. "Certain . . . two . . . showin' a badge . . ."

Gabe's hand tightened on the cup he was holding.

A badge.

His eyes jerked north. "Toe-shot," he whispered.

Bob Graffman and two more men rushed out of the hotel. Woody said something to them that Gabe couldn't hear, then they fanned, spreading around the plaza.

"Goddammit . . ." Gabe whispered.

Mitch and Zach were riding into a trap. One that he'd led them into.

He looked toward the river, then moved his eyes slowly back to the men walking around the plaza. Woody sitting down in front of the cantina. Candy leaning against the blacksmith barn. Graffman coming across the plaza. Morales edging through the wares in front of a shop.

Gabe set his cup on a table by the door and walked to his horse. He mounted the gray and turned him across the plaza.

"Company?" he called to Woody as he rode by.

"None of your affair," Sizemore said coldly. "Go find your grass growin'."

Behind Gabe, Reno called across the plaza. "They're comin' in, boss," he said, and stepped behind an adobe arch.

"So long," Woody said, and the way he said it was an order.

Nodding, Gabe rode out of the plaza and down the street toward the river. Halfway down the street, he reined the gray in. He could hear the water rushing over the rocks. A clean sound. A mountain sound. Not a part of the town. Behind him he could hear the sound of voices and horse hooves.

"Hell," he growled, "I can't even let Zach get it that way. One more time, Toe-shot."

Dismounting, he tied the gray to a small orange tree and jerked Stacker's Sharps from its scabbard. Loading it, he started the fifty yards back to the plaza.

Walking, he slipped the money from his coat pocket and stuffed it into his back pants pocket, then slipping the coat off, he tossed it aside.

Still walking, Gabe could see the tables in front of the cantina as they slipped into view. Unwinding the cartridge belt from around the stock of the Sharps, he slipped it over his shoulder, then resting the rifle on his shoulder, he unhooked his pistol.

Passing a woman making bread, he came up the hill and could see well into the plaza.

Mitch and Zach were already there. Riding past the well. Gabe frowned. They'd come quicker than he'd thought.

The deputy and the bearded man moved toward the hotel. Behind them Reno and Morales stepped into the open. Gabe's view of Woody was blocked by the cantina. Pressing closer to the building, Gabe edged up its side toward the plaza.

"Goddamn," Gabe heard a voice, "this one's a pup."

"I do believe you're right," someone laughed. "Must need lawdogs bad to steal 'em right out of their mothers' arms."

Gabe came up to the corner of the building. Mitch and Zach were still on horseback. Woody's men were in the open, coming into the plaza, forming a wide ring around the two men.

Cocking the Sharps, Gabe stepped around the corner.

"Woody," he said, and leveled the barrel of the rifle on the outlaw, "don't turn around." He raised his voice: "The rest of you," he shouted, "just stand still, or old Woody'll have a hole you can use as a wheel in his back." He half looked at the men on horseback. "Mitch," he said, "you and Zach—"

"Woody?" Bob Graffman came from behind the well.

"Do as he says," Sizemore snapped.

"You and Zach," Gabe repeated, "ride down this way."

Nodding, Mitch nudged his horse out slowly, taking him around the cantina tables. Zach followed.

"Zach—" Gabe started to say.

Bob Graffman sidestepped, getting Mitch between him and Gabe, drawing his gun. Gabe reeled, bringing the Sharps around. Woody Sizemore dived for the cover of the tables.

"Mitch," Gabe shouted.

The boy turned toward Graffman, trying to draw, when a shot slammed into his thigh. Still turning, Mitch screamed falling, tearing at the horse's reins, dragging the animal's head around and pitching both of them crashing into the tables.

As the horse fell, Gabe sited on Graffman running, and pulling the trigger, shattered his head in an explosion of blood.

Zach kicked free of his saddle, smashing into some chairs.

Mitch's horse lurched back to his feet, leaving the boy behind, stunned.

Drawing his pistol, Gabe ran toward the deputy, firing first at Sizemore scrambling around the side of the hotel, then at Reno and Jesus Morales.

Zach pushed himself to his feet.

"Get Mitch," Gabe yelled at him.

Shoving himself through the tables, Zach drew his gun and fired back into the plaza without aiming, then ran for Mitch.

Reno stood in the plaza firing. Kicking through the tables, Gabe shot him once in the chest, then again, driving him down into the dirt.

Zach made it to Mitch, and reaching down, he got his hand through the deputy's gunbelt and jerked him into a sitting position. Firing again, Gabe ran to the deputy, and grasping his arm, Zach took the other and they dragged him, charging for the door of the cantina.

Lead ripped at the wood of the tables and lashed across the wall in front of them.

Running, still hauling the deputy, Zach hit the door first, bursting through the old wood, shattering it, then fell rolling, with Mitch following him. Gabe let go of the boy, let him fall, and lunged to one side of the door. Slugs pounded into the wall.

Turning, Gabe caught a blur of movement across the room, and bringing his pistol up, he saw the woman. One of the hotel cooks.

"Get out of here," he screamed at her.

The woman turned, running behind the bar and down the back hall to the alley.

"Gonna kill her too?" Zach snapped.

"Christ, Zach, not now," Gabe barked, and turned to the

deputy twisted on the floor. His leg was bent crooked under him, his pants leg soaked with blood. He was still out from the fall.

"Toe-shot," Gabe whispered and knelt beside him.

The boy's head rolled.

At the door Zach yelled: "They're comin'."

Nodding, Gabe stood up. "Let's go," he said, pointing toward the back hall. "Carry him. I'll cover."

"Don't give me orders, you sonof—"

"Do it, goddammit, and maybe we'll get out of this alive. Or do you want to discuss it?"

The muscles flexed under Zach's beard, and frowning, he turned from the door, pulled the deputy up, and lifting him, hoisted him up on his back and held his arm with his left hand. In the other was his gun.

Gabe reloaded the Sharps and then his pistol.

"Yours," he said, handing Zach the pistol.

Zach stared back at him and slowly exchanged guns with him. Gabe loaded the second gun, and taking the deputy's from his holster, jammed it into his belt.

"Mitch," he shouted.

The deputy's head twitched slightly.

"Mitch," Gabe yelled again, "can you hear me?"

The deputy nodded faintly.

"Try and hold on," Gabe said to the boy, then went to the outside door of the bar. A scraping of wood from the door leading to the hotel brought Gabe's eyes and the Sharps around. Harper fired.

"Run," he ordered Zach, and hauling Mitch, the bearded man lumbered across the room. Keeping the Sharps on the hotel entrance, Gabe started backing for the hallway.

A form bolted into the street entrance, firing wildly. Bottles exploded behind the bar. Gabe swung the Sharps and shot the man, slamming him back out of the doorway into a wash of broken tables. Gabe drew Zach's gun and turned it to the hotel door, firing at a flicker of movement there, splintering frame wood and shattering a window in the lobby.

Zach ran down the hall. Still backing, Gabe followed him.

Dragging Mitch, Zach stumbled out of the hall and into the dirt.

Jesus Morales was waiting.

From the side of the building the Mexican fired, hitting the hotel's back stairs, blowing out a rung. Slumping to his knees, Zach twisted Mitch off his back and reeled toward Morales.

Coming into the alley to get clear of the stairs, Morales thumbed off another shot, geysering the dirt in front of the bearded man.

Still turning, Zach got off a wobbly shot, hitting the Mexican in the calf.

Dragging his foot, Morales fired again, blasting the wall behind Zach. The bearded man dropped to his chest and shot the Mexican in the shoulder, knocking him back and down. Morales sat hunched, then shaking his head, and lifting his glazed eyes, he thumbed the hammer of his pistol again.

"Damn you," Zach screamed, firing and missing.

Gabe stepped from the doorway and shot the Mexican twice in the chest, the first driving him back into the dirt, the second flattening him. Tossing the Sharps away, Gabe pulled the deputy's gun from his belt and handed it to Zach.

"Let's go," he said, and gripped the deputy under the arm. Zach wobbled to his feet staring at the bloody hulk.

"He wouldn't go down—"

"You're gonna kill a man—kill 'im, don't think. Now let's go."

Nodding, Zach turned and was leaning over to help Mitch when Woody, Candy, and another man came from around the hotel, running across the alley, firing.

Wheeling, Gabe shot the first man, sending him staggering into the others. Dodging the falling man, Candy got off one shot, pounding the wall behind Gabe.

Woody fired at Zach, hitting him in the arm, twisting him back around.

Ignoring the gunfire, Gabe stood sidewise and shot Candy in the stomach, sprawling him backward, and was turning to Woody when Zach came out of the dirt putting a shot through Woody's thigh, and Gabe smashed his hip, piling him back into the wall of the hotel, then to his knees.

Standing, Zach leveled his gun at Sizemore, stretching his arm out as if he wanted to pin the wounded man to the wall.

Woody struggled to raise his gun, and fell forward on his face.

Zach kept his gun on the downed man. Walking. Cocking the hammer.

"Zach," Gabe said.

Zach didn't hear him. He kept walking toward Sizemore writhing in the dirt.

"Zach—" Gabe screamed.

Behind them the hinge of the livery door moaned, and Zach wheeled like it had been a shot, bringing the gun around.

Running, Gabe dived at him, catching the bearded man in the hip with his shoulder and throwing the shot wild as both of them rolled in the dirt.

Gabe screamed, grasping his side, then sat up slowly.

"You sonofabitch," Zach raged, "there's—"

Miguel, the livery boy, stepped from behind the door.

"*Qué pasa?*" he asked, and saw the man with the gun.

Zach blinked, staring at the boy. Gabe pulled himself up stiffly. "Go home," he whispered to the boy. "Pronto."

Nodding and still staring at Zach, the livery boy went back down the alley and into the street.

"There were only seven," Gabe said to Zach.

Zach's eyes came up trembling. "I just turned," he tried to explain. "There wasn't time to—" and his words trailed as he realized what he was saying.

"Yeah," Gabe nodded, "I know," he said, and turned to Mitch.

Mitch struggled, sitting up in the dirt.

"Hello, Toe-shot," Gabe smiled, walking to the boy. "Let me get you some shade," he said leaning down, and somebody was on the other side helping him.

He looked up into Jenny's tear-wet face.

"Mornin', Miss Shannon," he nodded. "Rough day so far."

"You're a damn fool," she whispered, and they pulled the boy back against the wall of the hotel.

People began to merge into the alley. The hotel clerk's bald head poked out of the cantina hallway.

"You are well, señor?"

"Yeah," Gabe nodded. "Get a doctor, this boy—"

"I'm all right," Mitch protested. "Just my leg."

"Get that doctor," Gabe said, and looked at Woody, who was lying in the dirt but still breathing. "For this one too," Gabe nodded.

The clerk's head disappeared.

Gabe looked at the deputy again. "Looks like your wounds are movin' up."

"Gonna quit 'fore they get in the a—" he looked at Jenny, "in the behind," he cleared his throat.

"Hurt bad?"

Grimacing, Mitch nodded, "A little worse than tryin' to shoot my toe off."

Gabe smiled, then narrowed his eyes. "You serious about quittin'?"

Mitch nodded. "Yeah," he said, then added, "but it ain't because I'm scared."

Gabe's jaw pushed a smile through his face. "I know that."

Mitch's eyes fell, and he raised them again without shame. "I could have killed Zach back out there. I had him cold. I couldn't do it."

Gabe looked back at Zach. He had gotten up and was sit-

ting on a bench in front of the bathhouse. His arm was bleeding, but he stared forward into the dirt.

Gabe brought his eyes back to the deputy. "I'm glad,
Mitch," he said, and stood up. "So long."

"You leavin' now? You're hurt, you damn hard-headed old
man."

"Goin' while I can," Gabe nodded.

Mitch nodded reluctantly. "So long, Gabe."

The old lawman's eyes moved to the woman. His hand
touched his vest pocket.

"One for Lucky Callahan," she said.

Gabe smiled. "Two," he said, and turned back down the
alley.

In front of the bathhouse, Zach Harper stretched up to his
feet, waiting. Gabe walked until there was ten feet left between them and halted.

The bearded man's eyes met Gabe's with an odd knowing
and a fear of it.

"I'm leavin'," Gabe said.

Zach moved, striding out, walking deliberately, his eyes
fixed on Gabe's. The sound of his boots filled Gabe, and it
seemed like Zach came for a long time. He stopped square in
front of Gabe. The bearded man's hand gathered at his side.
Clinching so tight it trembled. And trembling, opened again.
His eyes flicked to the barn door and slowly back.

He brushed by Gabe and walked to where Gabe had
thrown Stacker's Sharps. Leaning down, he picked the rifle
gently out of the dirt. He stood staring at it, then without
looking back, he walked into the hallway to the bar.

Gabe watched him, then let his eyes linger on the woman
and the boy. Turning quickly, he walked to the street and
toward the river.

Two men helped Mitch to his feet.

"Down there," he gestured the way Gabe had gone.

Holding onto the men, and with Jenny beside him, he made his way to the street.

Gabe was crossing the river, pushing the gray to the other side, leaning slightly to one side. They came up on the bank and Gabe turned the horse toward the mountains. Heat waves rose up around him as he rode, and he seemed to float. Hovering.

Mitch looked at Jenny. Her eyes stayed with the man as he rode for a long time, then pulled reluctantly away.

"Time," she whispered.

He looked back to the man on the horse for a moment. Riding. Mingling into the heat bands. Blending toward the peaks. Endlessly riding.

"Yeah," he sighed.

"Are you all right?" Jenny asked.

Mitch glanced at her, then eased his eyes back to Gabe. "I am now," he nodded, watching the rider until he was lost in the distance.

Turning, he tried to smile. "Just saying goodbye," he whispered softly and started back up the street.

DATE DUE

School Specialty Supply, Inc. 13-517-585 (No. 393)

MY 21 '80	9125		JK
JE 16 '80			
AG 18 '80			
NO 10 '80			
AG 12 '81			
AP 14 '84			
MR 20 '85			
OC 9 '85			
MR 13 '86			
AP 2			

BURNLEY MEMORIAL LIBRARY
(Falls Township)
Cottonwood Falls, Kansas

1. Books may be kept two weeks and renewed once for the same period, except magazines, which may be kept four days.

2. A fine of two cents per day will be charged on each book which is not returned according to rule above. No book will be issued to any person incurring such a fine until it has been paid.

3. All injuries to books beyond reasonable wear and all losses shall be made good to the satisfaction of the librarian.

4. Each borrower is held responsible for all books drawn on his card and for all fines accruing on the same.

DEMCO